To Martha
and Tony —
Thanks for
everything and
Hope you enjoy.
— Dave Tilton

TO
LEAVE
BEFORE
THE
SUN

DONKEY HOTEL PRESS : 2007

Donkey Hotel Press: San Francisco, Vallejo, Antioch:
"we'll leave the lit on for you"

Here's our shiny ISBN:
978-0-6151-7997-1

Two Novellas of California's Central Valley

FIRST
TO
LEAVE

LEWIS
BUZBEE

ZACHARIAH

Taylor Macoby sat on his haunches on the edge of the cotton field and knew that the land had passed him by again, knew that it had never been his and never would be. He did not allow himself to think too long on the latter because that thought might stop him here on this dead land and keep him from moving, strand him. When he had brought his wife, two sons, and baby daughter to Oklahoma from Texas, he had done so because he had heard there was share land available and that you could work your way to buying it. In 1900, his father and mother had moved the family from Virginia to Texas on the same promise. Always the promise, the land would be yours.

He scratched his name in the dirt with a broken hollow branch and gently blew on the dust until his name disappeared. He saw and knew and directed the irony of the gesture, and in that gesture and the knowing of it lay the certainty of the family moving again. He had stopped hoping and began to make fun of himself and his place in the world.

The land, the red and gray countries of Oklahoma, had passed over everyone this time. They had worked it to death. There was no topsoil left, none at all. Dust. He had never been much of a farmer and because of this he was able to see the end before the others. Hope did not blind him to the land's demise, while the others still thought things would get better. *Rain*, they would say, huddled after church, *all we need is a good rain*. But rain would not bring dirt; the dirt would never return. The other sharecroppers needed hope to get by, but Zack did not. Farming was what he had always done to feed his family. He might wildcat the rigs, but that was not a family job, and as much as he had considered leaving the family to work the rigs, sending money home every month, he knew he would never go back to them once he left and knew the checks would stop arriving in the mail. Hope clouded your mind. Everyone would leave the land soon. Most would wait until the end, when they were evicted from the land they thought had been theirs because they had worked it, and then there would be trouble and hardship and a scramble for the last piece of land in the next place. Zack would leave now, tell no one. Get to the new place first.

He smoothed down the corners of his silver and yellow moustache. He wiped the infuriating dust from his boots and stood with a liberating groan. There, he thought to himself, job done. Once he had made up his mind to leave, it was as if he had already left the empty buildings behind. He would have to talk to Eva about it, but she would not argue. She would take it up as her idea, in the end, and make the doing of it easier. Eva had never liked this place. *Why would anyone in their right mind want to live here,* she had asked when she first stepped down on the place two years before, and she had continued to ask that question almost every day since, standing at the kitchen sink, looking out at the bluff of trees that followed the high watercourse along the blurry western edge of their share. She asked the question, he thought, not because the land was so wretched, although it was, and not because the light here was dull and their prospects, too, although they were, but as a preparation for the next move, a way of keeping herself from sitting down in the place and getting too comfortable. Her family had also moved from Virginia to the same gulf town in Texas, where she and Zack had met and courted. She was used to moving, and when she first saw the gray country of Oklahoma, had made up her mind to stay used to it. The oil rigs scattered about them, she had told Zack, looked like mosquitoes sucking the blood from the land. *They* belonged on this land.

The sun set red and hazy, a feeble shade of orange on the scarred earth, threatening to be beautiful, as if the land's last effort to hold him. *Sailor's delight,* he whispered. He turned to the house from behind which the oil rigs loomed. Thin smoke leaked from the kitchen chimney. His sons, Nimion and Elwell, played soldiers in the yard; Nimion, thirteen, shouldered a squirrel gun, while Elwell, ten, brandished a carved stick. Nimion was too old to play soldier. When the family left here, both boys would have to quit school, the cropping too hard to do alone anymore.

Eva watched him from the kitchen window. With no ounce of recognition, they stared at each other. Zack broke off first and headed for the water pump.

"You heard from your cousins in California?" he asked at dinner between sips of the greens' soup.

"Got that letter last month," she said. The children ate in silence, as required.

"That's right," he said, drying his moustache. "I forgot. How are they doing out there?"

"They're good, Lord willing," she said, unmovable.

He knew she would not give him what he wanted unless he asked for it first, until he succumbed and invited her into the decision, instead of inviting herself in, as he would have it. She had figured this out about him years ago, that he would prefer she initiate every discussion, since she seemed to know of it in advance anyway, but she grew stubborn in her knowledge of him and refused to speak first.

"Do they like it there?" he asked, setting his napkin next to his bowl of soup and placing both hands on the table. "Are there opportunities for them?"

"Plenty of opportunity," she said. She swatted the boy Elwell with her napkin.

Elwell looked up, stunned, mouth opened to question. His father pointed at him, a warning.

"Tell me," he said, looking out the warped kitchen windows. "Do you think they might know of anything out there for us?"

"They might," she said. "They just might. She was mentioning some farms for sale at real cheap up around Modesto. Said the land was good, growing anything thanks to irrigation."

"I've been thinking," he said.

She smiled on her spoon, and he knew that this was what she had been waiting for, the invitation she had demanded of him, for she had probably seen him out near the field's edge, squatting and thinking about leaving, and she had probably known then what he had decided, probably could have started packing.

"Yes," she said.

"You know we can't stay here, he said. "It's the dirt; there ain't any."

"I know," she said. "I don't know why anyone in their right mind would want to live here."

Just to be able to say that again, he thought, one last time. She might have pushed him this far for the joy of repeating that phrase one last time.

"I was thinking California, then," he said, ladling the soup, wishing there were something else to eat, thinking about the overlade tables of California. "I was thinking there wasn't anyplace else to go."

"Yes," she said. "I'll write to them tonight; you can take it in tomorrow."

That night, while she scribbled on an old piece of school paper one of the children had brought home, and fashioned an envelope out of another piece of it, he went out to the barn to drink and walk around and figure.

He hated this place, reaching up and behind the corner post of the barn, pulling out the bottle, hated this place because he had to hide his bottle out here, because it was a dry county in the middle of Prohibition and he couldn't bear the kind of self-righteous hypocrisy that went along with a dry county at any time. He reached farther back behind the post and found the tobacco. He took a long pull on the bottle; the liquor was clear as water, dry and burning as the land. He rolled a cigarette and stuck that one behind his ear and rolled another one and walked out into the clear night and lit it.

He had sat in the church, dog tired on Sundays, and listened to the preacher rant about the devil-drink and whore's tobacco, wishing the whole time he could have a swig and a smoke right there with his feet propped up on the pews. He listened to other farmers and the farmers' wives exclaim and shout at Satan and command those vile vices to be gone. He talked with the other men after the service, standing in the godless sun, while the men, inspired by the preaching--the swaying rhythms of the sermon and the singing and the breath-filled organ, the clashing tambourines--went on about the evils of practically everything but especially smoke and drink, and of course, fornication. But he had also been there, when, on the same day, on the Lord's day, presumably with Him watching, these same men had snuck away from dinners and weddings and such and gone round the back of the house to have a snort and a smoke, and he had been there on those same days when the same men had snuck off into the scrub with other men's daughters.

The moon set thin and crippled. The dogwoods that marked the watercourse and the boundary looked in the feeble night like a train of refugees, bent people moving on with hopeless hope to another place, dragging their overburdened carts. If he waited much longer, he would be one of these people, dragging his life behind him, sheeplike with the others. He drew heavily on the cigarette, then leaned his head far back and gazed up at the dim sky as if the answers were inscribed there, and exhaled the blue smoke through pursed lips. He pulled the bottle from his pocket, tossed the cork high into the air and off into the scrub and guzzled. The warmth invaded his chest and head until his brain gave way and loosened.

It had seemed to him in the beginning of his marriage that it, meaning his life, would be easier than this. That sense of ease was the deceit of his wedding and honeymoon. Briefly he'd imagined that life would always be as it had been on the beach for those few days, as though all the difficulties and boredoms of his life before that had been a test he had endured, and that when the preacher pronounced them married that tedious life was forever behind him, understanding, he thought for a moment, why people got married and started families. All the time he was alone, until he was almost forty, working hard at scratching and for nothing, had been nearly unendurable, the point of it being the few hours at night and the most of Sunday when he could stop and be away from his life. When he met Eva, and she put forward the idea that they get married and he had agreed to that, saying almost anything to her at the time so that his few free hours might be spent with her, a woman much younger than himself, he suspected he said yes to her for a purpose other than convincing her to lie with him, suspecting that working hard with someone else might be easier than the constant loneliness. She had a charm about her that was not easily understood by his brothers, nor in the beginning by himself when he thought of her as female company. She was young, yes, that was always desirable, eighteen when he first courted her, and so her body was still fresh, if not a little stocky. Her face was what her own mother referred to as "horsey," but in her face, in her thick jaw and especially in her brooding eyes, was a lightness he could not explain to anyone, even to her, so he never tried, and in that lightness he saw some hope for surcease from the weariness that had plagued him so long.

Eva was the younger sister of a family that had become wedded to his family years before, when his family, the Macobys, came to the Texas gulf. The Crumes worked the next share over and had several daughters, two of which, Effie and Ophelia, as they came of age, married two Taylor boys, Zack's older brothers Milford and Eugene. There had been a lot of joking over the years about the destiny of Zack and Eva, the two youngest children of the families, but when Zack first met Eva she was all of two years old.

As though the jokes were seeds unwittingly planted in their lives, borne by some hot wind, the idea seemed to take root. Zack never married, hardly having the chance to meet anyone else in that barren place, except at church where everyone else had already married, and no new families moved into the area the land was so poor. As Eva moved away from childhood, he began to look at her differently. Finally, after many years of ignoring him as a pesky uncle, Eva, when she was sixteen, started to look at him differently, too, telling him later that it was his eyes, sandy blue, and his shock of already gray hair, those lights in the dark red face, that had captured her. And the way he had looked at her. But she did not give in to his caresses and suggestions until she was eighteen, and when she did, he knew immediately, even though she would be the first to bring it up, he knew that they would marry, even as he mounted her for the first time there on the beach where they would later honeymoon, knew as he came inside of her, looking down on her and recognizing the strange light in her dark, horsey face. A week later she put forth the notion that they marry, but she would not let it go at that, maneuvering him so that he had to say the words, ask the question as though it were his idea, so she could agree, as though she were surprised by it.

It was in the weeks before and after their marriage that he had lived for the first time with the hope that life would relent and grant him a gift.

They married in the flat church on the flat ground of Texas, the intertwined families present and joyous, thrilled that the youngest had finally been squared away and the raising and providing for the next crop of children, already present and squealing, could continue. The wagon was loaded with the greatest munificence Zack had ever seen larded onto two people. The horses had been combed and braided with ribbons, and the best of the horses, too, the riding horses, the finest from each family. In the back of the wagon were baskets and baskets of food, chickens and greens and even fresh fruits. Zack had not seen or heard of some of these fruits, and gazing upon them as if they were rare gems, had no idea how his family had obtained them. Zack and Eva drove off, chased by screams and children for a quarter mile, and then they drove in silence for the rest of the day until they got to the beach and had to decide which dune looked best to them both. This was late spring. The weather was clear and warm and dry, the perfect time before the arduous heat of summer's harvest. White clouds as round as horses' rumps rolled by.

Zack unloaded the heavy wagon, while Eva went off into the dunes to gather herbs. He dug a fire pit protected from the wind in the center of three dunes, and set out their bedding and utensils. Eva returned with an armload of sage, fennel, and rosemary, and some broad, wet palm leaves. She made dinner, while Zack fed and watered the horses.

Eva crushed the herbs and stuffed them under the skin of the chickens, then skewered the chickens and roasted them high and slow. She dropped butter-stuffed potatoes directly into the fire, and wrapped whole corns in the palm leaves and steamed them on the edge of the pit. She slit open a loaf of hard bread and filled it with crushed garlic and more butter and set it on top of the corn where one side cooked crunchy and almost black, the other soft and moist.

After tending the horses, Zack sat on the top of one of the dunes and watched Eva make dinner, and looked out over the sky-blue sea. She took her time with each movement, loving the food, and in that loving she shaped the way it would taste. He could almost taste everything as she put it on the fire, especially the fatty, cracked and cooked skin of the chicken. He realized at that moment that he had no idea who this woman was, had not had the time to even think of who she might be, and now they were joined in a family and it was too late if he did not like what he might learn about her. Her dark solemn face, thick lips and hooked nose--the nose he saw in his three children--enticed him because they contrasted so with her pale eyes, eyes like his own, he thought. He slumped down in the sand and watched her work, the warmed sand gathered around him, and he saw nothing then but her hands and wrists as they worked the food to something he could never make of it, and he watched her face, full of furious attention, yet somehow relaxed and enjoying the day, and then, for the first time in his adult life, he fell asleep with the sun soaking his face, luxuriating in that day and the dunes and the possibility of that new life, wrapped in the braided aromas of the cookout.

They ate dinner greedily, grease and juices on their fingers and chins, the herb smells permeating everything, swallowed into them as if they had eaten the soft dunes and the ragged plants that grew there. They washed down dinner with a bottle of red wine, Chianti, which he pronounced as giant-eye, and she laughed and swatted him. He had never had wine before, not even in church where they used grape juice for the Savior's blood. They fell into the wine's soft glow and were soon making love, naked in the dusk, the ocean at low tide hushing behind them. They pulled the pleasure from each other slowly, lingering. He had never had so much time. The first time they made love, he had not noticed in his haste exactly how curved her body was, had not noticed that her breasts seemed to stand out and away from her body as he tugged on them with his teeth, and how much pleasure that seemed to give her. He saw that she also took pleasure in their lovemaking.

Zack tromped around naked except for his boots, collecting wood and building up the fire, while she laughed at him and he posed for her. After dinner, while they cleaned up the dinner mess, they looked at each other, incredulous, and stopped their cleaning, knowing that no one cared whether they cleaned and that they had only done so out of a deep and fierce habit. She talked to him, as they lay in the dusk, wrapped in old quilts and blankets. A moonless night, a thick soup of stars.

"Our own place," was her keystone, hushed over and over again in the dark night miles from anyone, hushed as if everyone were listening, hushed under her breath, close to his neck, hushed to protect the idea from being stolen, as if they had been the first to think of it, as if there were forces in the world that would steal it from them.

Yes, he thought, years later, standing in the yard, waiting to leave again, they would steal it from them, as if they, the forces of the world, whoever or whatever they were, had been there that night in the dunes, had heard their hushed secrets, and began at that moment to stalk them.

"Our own place," she had whispered on the beach. He told her yes, they would have their own place, not next year or the year after, and not in Texas certainly, but somewhere and soon.

"Together," she said. "Together." They could do anything together, she knew deep inside of her. She made him promise; he did so readily, believing that night, for the first time, that it was possible, that stepping outside of their difficult lives for this one day and night of lying in the dunes offered them enough of a respite to imagine a different kind of life, and that imagining that life was enough to make it happen. Her voice soothed him and pulled from him words he did not know he possessed, telling her yes and describing what their place would look like and how it would come about, and how they would keep it, inventing plans already to stave off the typical disasters, plague and drought and flood. Her voice lulled him into the other world, but in the lulling and soothing, she caused him to leap forward and imagine beyond his life, her voice a strange, comforting prod, then her hands on him again and their making love to the slow tides.

The next morning, after coffee and bread and dates, they rode the horses bareback along the beach for miles, talking and close, then silent and far away, then at a full gallop, for she surprised him by kicking her horse and loving the speed of it, laughing and kicking down the beach.

He caught a flounder on a cast line and a crab in a cage. Eva boiled and cracked the crab, which they ate on the hard bread, washed down with more wine. She made a bed of herbs for the flounder, wrapped it in palm leaves and steamed it next to the fire for a few minutes, then at the last second set it directly on the fire until the palms burned. More potatoes and corn and wine, then coffee. They made love until sunset, then packed up and rode back to the farm, she asleep with her head on his lap by the time they arrived, no one but the dogs to greet them.

Now, under the famished Oklahoma moon, he remembered it all, the only time he had rested. He conjured the smell of burning fennel, that pungent licorice, and the whole trip came back to him and he tried to grab it and hold onto it, but it kept slipping away, washed away by the torrent of years and work that came after. Their beach dreams didn't even last until the first child, Nimion, was born, only nine months after the honeymoon. They had rented their own share, nine miles north and east, and immediately the work had started to kill them, the long hours and days. Before dawn and until after dark they both worked, Eva pregnant, and there was not any chicken with herbs, or crab, or flounder, but greens and flour and sometimes potatoes. There was only the scrawny mule to help, and the solace, on market days, of a bottle Zack shared with no one.

He had been the first to stop talking, grunting in answer to her questions, then finally a hard silence, and then she had stopped talking, her dark face clouded by his surrender. She yelled at him once, only once, that he had been the first to give up. They communicated in code, short cryptic civilized messages, each barbed and poisonous. For a long time he forgot about their honeymoon, it had become too painful a memory in its sweetness, but in the last few years he had begun to remember it again, when he'd been drinking, wishing he could find some woman as young as Eva had been once.

That was where he stood now, in the bleak heart of Oklahoma, *a fucking desert*, thinking back on the beach honeymoon, wishing he were there, but drinking instead and trying to remember it all. When he finished the bottle he tossed it far off into the night where it thudded against a piece of earth so dull it didn't shatter the cheap glass. He found the bottle in the dust and flung it out again into the night, where it did break, and the memory he had tried so hard to capture, shattered, too, into a thousand pieces, and he slumped to the ground he hated.

EVA found him there in the beige dawn, asleep on his back, mouth open and dried. She pulled him awake and gave him a cup of water, then led him into the house, where he sat at the kitchen table and drank coffee all day long, not going into the fields because that work, which was normally futile, was now superfluous.

They were gone already, removed, it was only a matter of how, and that required thinking, even with his brain as thick as mush. She worked around him and waited. He got up and left a few days later, without a word, when the morning was red and troubled.

Six dollars and fifty cents. In the long run that's what it would cost them to move to California, so he would have to make that work. That's what she had hidden in the back of one of the dresser drawers, stuck up behind the old newspaper, thirteen half-dollar pieces. He had always known where she hid the money--her money because he never kept money longer than the next bottle. He always knew when she added more to the cache, or removed some for a new coat for one of the children before the coat arrived. He knew she had added or subtracted, as if the air around the money were a fine dust that telegraphed her most careful movements. Just as she always knew where he hid his booze and his tobacco and how much was there and when he drank, and she knew this not from watching him and smelling him and putting up with him, but from sensing, the way he sensed her, the disturbance of the air around everything, the tension they both carried when hiding things. Yet neither would admit to what secrets they knew. They buried their secrets deepest of all their possessions.

He took the thirteen half dollars, not caring whether she found him at it or not, with her in the next room mending quietly. He had one more cup of coffee and left, not having to say anything, he knew, for they had been through this before. He had left wordlessly on several occasions when the family needed more money than was there, leaving with what little money they had saved and returning several days later with more, always just enough. She could not have questioned him, even if she thought he might answer. The money appeared and that was the only necessary discussion. She watched him urge the red mule into the endless morning.

"Will you never talk?" she asked the still air of the dusty kitchen.

The six dollars and fifty cents had to grow to at least one hundred. Zack's only thought, as he rode off the farm the penultimate time, was that he would lose the mule and take the train, but he had not gotten further than that. The mule, which he kicked and struck with a switch, knowing he could push it beyond its limits, to its death if needed, the mule rocked beneath him. Zack regarded the limitless horizon as though the answer lay there. Unable to think in the front of his brain about where he was going, he pushed everything to the back of his brain so it could do its work; eventually that secret thinking would provide him with an answer. In the meantime, he kept the front of his brain occupied with thoughts of her and what she did and did not know about his exploits.

He assumed that she knew more than she could, or pretended to. When he returned from his *little trips*, imagining that was what she called them, imagining the bite on those words, she'd have a smug air about her, as if she had known all along, even before he'd done it, what he would do. He also knew that she knew only the essence of what he did, never the specifics, for that was where her smugness came from, her knowing that essentially what he had done was illegal or unethical, beyond the standards of propriety. She lorded her superiority over him upon his return the way she ladled out the soup to him, in the way she dressed the kids in the morning or fed the chickens, performing each part of her day with a fastidious deliberation. But she always took the money, which he laid on the table, in the open, without explanation. The secret of how he got the money was so much bigger than the secret of the money itself it seemed silly to both of them to slip the money into the dresser again. That was *his* superiority, how he lorded it over her, barbarous, unashamed of what he had done, keeping his family intact one more time. Riding the dead tired mule through the cadaverous landscape, he laughed at their jousting.

His *little trips* had saved them from Texas. The share land there had given up. Some of the family had moved on to Oklahoma already, and some, foolishly he believed, back to Virginia as if they would find the land there as it was before, plentiful, up for grabs.

None of the excuses and explanations and plans the other men reported and formulated after church services did any good to save them from Texas. They were still going down the hard way. Zack saw it in the faces of the children, which were sallow, sickly, as yellow as the land and the burnt Texas sky. So he took one of his *little trips*, taking two dollars and a wagon and a mule, and a plan for moving to Oklahoma tucked under his hat, though a different corner of Oklahoma than their families had chosen, as if their families were part of the forces that seemed determined to take the simplest things away from them. He came back from his *little trip* with changed eyes. Zack and Eva and the children left Texas without a goodbye.

He imagined what she imagined of his forays into the world. He saw her sitting on the porch steps and wishing she had a rocker to sit in. He knew she chewed tobacco when he was gone, from the stains on her teeth and fingers. She saw him riding a fast white horse, chasing down a train, pistols drawn; or she saw him stride into a bank and casually rob it with a cloaked head and a hand that never left its pocket; or she saw him high in the mountains robbing an Indian grave of its gold pieces, taking one intricate piece at a time and taking only what he needed. Stories from the tired magazines she read over and over. All these imaginings accompanied him through the bleak day and bleaker landscape on the half day's ride to the railroad crossing where the cotton and other crops were loaded.

Late in the afternoon, one farm shy of the crossing, he sold the mule, broken as it was, to a white, harmless-looking farmer, an owner of some small piece of land. Zack looked into the man's pudgy pink face and envied and hated him for his ownership, no matter how meager, Zack thinking that, simply by owning that twisted land that it had to be a better piece of land. He felt contemptuous of and superior to this man, whom he perceived as nothing short of dull and nearly dead, whereas Zack himself was brazen and outlandish.

Zack found the man out by his barn, surveying his acres in the buttermilk afternoon, and he weaved for the man a careful tale of woe.

"Just need to get rid of it," he said, looking off. "Headed for the rail crossing. Like to get there before evening."

"Where you headed?" asked the landowner.

"Folks. Virginia," letting those words and that distance hang there and tell the story.

"Problems?" asked the other man, straightening out of his pudgy droop and putting his hands in his pockets, as if shoring himself against the dire news, as if his own relations were the story's subject.

"Mother," said Zack. "Not bad, just gotta be there."

Zack hunkered down, squatting on his haunches, letting the other man be bigger than he was, stronger, capable, as Zack was not, of standing up to the pressure of the woes and the sun and the gravity of the day. The landowner began to speak, and in that exhale, and because Zack knew how this story worked, Zack interrupted him and cut short the man's sympathy as if to say that that was enough, for in another moment Zack might break down and actually cry in front of a man.

"Mule don't look like much," he said. "Kind of beat-up looking, I know."

Zack stood.

"But she can work, I can tell you," he said, removing his hat and wiping his brow, the mere thought of how much farmland this animal had plowed making him sweat. The mule seemed sturdier at that moment to both men.

"I can give you thirty dollars," said the man, looking as far away as the curve of the earth would allow, offering half of what the mule might get in time and twice as much as the minimum Zack carried in his head.

"Well," said Zack, drawing out the word, closing his eyes, telling the man in that long syllable that the offer made was just the amount of money Zack needed to make his arduous journey, but that any decent man, a Christian man, would give Zack a little more to ease his burden.

"I can give you thirty-five," the man said, searching the horizon.

"You are a Christian gentleman, sir," said Zack, shaking the man's hand. "We are all obliged."

Zack did not refuse the buggy ride to the railroad crossing, delighted to discover that the landowner's son would be driving and he would not have to continue his mournful facade. He fingered the coins and bills that the farmer had given him and felt for the lump of his own money wrapped tight in his coat pocket. He delighted in the roundness of the coins. Zack got down at the crossing and took the bundle of food the landowner's wife had prepared for him--it seemed they'd never let him leave that squalid, little farm--and waved the buggy off.

Easy as that, he thought, waving. *Couldn't be easier.*

He ate in the shade of one of the warehouses, half a mile down the track from where the rusted train was loading. He imagined again what Eva would be thinking of him, at home having a chew or pushing the kids to bed, and knew that behind all his imaginings of Eva's thoughts, the plan was beginning to form. Each time he accidentally dipped in to bring that plan to the surface, he concentrated on Eva, for the plan, he knew, had to develop of its own and with plenty of time. He didn't want to interfere with himself.

Evening gave way to incessant night; the train pulled away from the yard. Zack appeared from out of nowhere and ran down the train, headed for an open car. In front of him, one car down, another man, bundle flying, ran along the train at the same pace and angle. Both men hit the train and waved to each other before ducking into the empty boxcars. Zack had spotted the man's bundle, and suspecting good things in it, climbed the side of the moving car and worked his way to the car behind.

"Loren," said the man.

"Zack."

Zack knew that the other man--younger, intelligent looking, dressed in worn but nice clothes, not farmer's clothes--was suspicious of him. Loren carried a knapsack, going somewhere, with a purpose, no matter how vague; Zack carried nothing and might have been on the lam, dangerous.

Zack rolled a quarter between him thumb and forefinger.

"I'd give you a quarter for a smoke," he said.

Loren and Zack made a deal. Zack gave him fifty cents for a shared half of a bottle, some tobacco and papers. Loren was clearly relieved to be holding currency again, and Zack was delighted, sucking back a quarter of his first cigarette on the first draw. Zack felt charitable giving up the fifty cents, reckoning that fifty cents to be part of the extra five dollars he'd connived from the farmer, as if somehow his charity toward Loren compensated for his earlier con. He remembered for a long time to come that he had given Loren more money than was necessary.

Both men were relieved to discover that neither had an urge to talk, so they drank and smoked and watched the blue story of the night roll past, the flat unsparing Oklahoma diorama with no moon visible to them. Zack shared his bread and jerky with Loren, then both men had one last smoke and crawled into opposite corners of the huge car and slept.

In the morning, as dawn ledged into view, Loren woke Zack and urged him to move quickly. The train was slowing.

"We're coming into Norman now," he said, kicking Zack softly in the ribs. "Up and at 'em, Adam. They find you here and they'll kick you bloody for the fun of it. Go."

Loren was gone. Zack stumbled up, cleared his head of uncertain dreams, jumped from the slowing train and rolled in the gravel, where he lay for a moment, wishing the gravel soft enough for sleep, but the ground did not give way. Zack sat up, thinking of coffee. He rolled a cigarette, thinking of biscuits in gravy, then he remembered the money in his pocket and the cigarette tasted less bitter on his tongue.

The deep morning that spread over Norman was as beautiful as Oklahoma had ever been to him, a tinge of red and pink in the eastern sky where the sun struggled. Past the rail yards the city began its rise from the crooked streets of the poorer neighborhoods to the high, lushly treed bluffs that overlooked the meager valley. Norman was as Zack remembered. He had passed through on one of his earlier trips and at that time made note of the bluffs above the city and those possibilities. Two days until Sunday, he was thinking, and in thinking that and watching the bluffs he knew that the plan in its particulars had formed. Smoking the last dregs of the first cigarette, he slapped the dust from his pants with his hat and set off towards town, walking fearlessly through the teeming rail yard.

The outlying districts of Norman were unpaved, and the dirt, trodden and parched, was like flour underfoot. The rickety houses leaned into the earth as if fatigued, the wood stretched and flaking. Newspaper and catalog pages blinded windows. Dogs trailed along every fence. Horses were tied up in backyards, chickens nagging their legs, laundry flag-like in the stiff air of the morning. The sky gave way to soot. Groups of children, shoeless and dirty, squealed their way to school, tugging and punching one another. Tired women worked over galvanized tubs, their husbands gone to work hours before, or thought Zack with a malicious smile, still in bed and hungover.

There had been many occasions on which Zack, staring out at the stupid land, unable any longer to fathom coaxing a living from it, pondered moving into town, maybe not Norman, but where seemed hardly to matter. He tried to imagine the type of work he'd find, maybe on the railroad, maybe in a factory, a vague image of himself pulling anonymous levers. He pictured a house and yard and porch. Town life had always appealed to Zack as the easier life, a life born to other people, but his imagination always stalled. He used blurred pictures of town life as a panacea against boredom, bloodied hands, and a stiff back.

The border between Norman's poor, white neighborhood and the colored neighborhood was a thick, close street of old hotels and bars and diners. *Driftersburg,* Zack dubbed it, *Wanderville, Ignoreland. My kind of place.*

At Bascom's Diner Zack ate eggs and potatoes, and sipped coffee from a thick, white mug. He sat at the counter and watched himself in the blemished mirror, while he smoked a cigarette and waited for his food to settle. He ordered another plate of eggs, this time with a thick slab of ham steak. He smoked another cigarette.

The owner of the diner, Bascom, "chief cook and bottle washer," was an angular fellow, shaved bald, who talked endlessly to Zack, as though Zack, exhibiting the good taste to have enough money for a meal, were entitled to some entertainment. Zack listened--smiling, smoking, nodding--and all the while watched the reflection of the diner in the mirror. Bascom spoke of his time in France in the Great War, peppering his talk with *guys like us,* as though he and Zack had been in the trenches together, though Zack suspected Bascom was a little too old to have seen any real action in the war, except the battle between the ham and eggs. There was too much fond memory of the war in Bascom's voice. One of Zack's brothers had been to France, and he hardly ever spoke of the war, or anything else, throwing himself into his farming.

Zack watched the other men in the diner. They were all out of work and had come here not to look for work, but to stare into their coffee and pretend to look for work. They were men waiting for a boom.

Bascom talked on at Zack, and while Zack would have appreciated silence, he also knew that part of his plan included someone like Bascom, a townsperson who would pretend that he had known Zack his whole life, someone to avert suspicions should they arise. Zack jingled the coins in his pockets when he paid for his meal so Bascom would see that he was a substantial man. Bascom winked at Zack to ensure their secret. Zack could almost see the manufacture in Bascom's head of the new stories of The Great War that would include Zack. Zack promised to be back for lunch.

The mote-filled main street of *Driftersburg* led to downtown Norman, where suddenly the streets were paved, and cars and buses began to appear. The houses were brick now, the streets lined with trees. Zack was grateful for the shade, a commodity almost as precious as water. Farther along, he came to the town square with its whitewashed band shell. Norman was the right size, small enough to cross and leave in a few minutes, big enough to get lost in. He walked with his head bent and as if with a purpose. He knew that seeming to have a purpose was as good as having one.

He passed banks and shops, glanced in their windows, consuming with quick glimpses all that might be seen through the clean, beveled-glass windows etched with frosty letters--the people and their costumes and their smiles and the little days they were having. It was such a clean world, everyone washed and starched, a world of substance; Zack felt that his life, his share life, was only some minor apparition of what a real life ought to be, a real life like the ones played out before him on this hive-like street with its orange and gray streetcar clanging past and the people so fitted to their transactions. As he walked along the street--he could not prevent himself from doing it even as he mumbled to himself that he should stop it--Zack continually touched the brim of his hat with his thumb and forefinger and lifted it a fraction of an inch off his head. He knew that this was his giveaway, his sign to others that he did not belong in this new town but on the farm, struggling in the dust. He felt like the bachelor wolf, making his obeisance to the silver-chested elders. *Hayseed*, he thought to himself, though he had been called worse. *Hick*.

The loathing he felt for his own life was swallowed, and thus compounded by, his yearning to be part of this clean and well-laundered life, this white-shirted life. He imagined himself in the bank, in a brand new suit, that woman there, the blonde with the red lipstick, her at his side, making a deposit. As if to atone for the sin of even thinking this, the nervous tipping of his hat became mechanical and precise. He tipped to everyone and everything.

He left the squat downtown and walked uphill, where he entered a residential neighborhood, and his anxieties doubled. Here the houses were beyond any realm he had ever seen before, stately homes as huge as wooden ships all set down together in the middle of the continent, as if washed there by a flood of Biblical proportions. It was for these homes that he had come to Norman, but their scale was much grander than he had imagined. Even the trees were more substantial, ancient trees in a new world. He tipped his hat to the trees that whispered back to him in the feather winds.

He walked to the top of the hills above Norman, walking quickly to avoid the inhospitable glares of the gardeners. The city was below him, comprehensible from this vantage, small enough to hold in his hands. The day clouded over, cooling. Zack took quick, careful note of two of the larger houses and walked purposefully down the hill and through the town, back to his side. He found a hotel that was cheap and creaky on a loud and dubious street. He had two entire days, two long nights.

Zack returned to Bascom's Diner, where he sipped coffee and listened to the foolish bald man tell him war stories. It seemed to Zack that Bascom had seen more various actions than anyone else in the war. "You're a modest man, Bascom," Zack told him, and Bascom half blushed, incredulous at his own humble nature. Zack protested that he was not hungry, but Bascom insisted that he have one of his famous Hamburg steaks, and even though Zack continued to protest, holding up his weathered hand, Bascom continued to insist and prepared the steak for him and would not think of accepting payment from his close friend. The diner was crowded, but Zack sat alone at the counter.

Zack, knowing it was his due, began to tell Bascom a little about himself. The bald cook leaned on out-turned arms, one hand gripping a spatula. Zack sopped up the hamburger gravy with a piece of bread. He told Bascom that he had come to Norman from Fayetteville, Arkansas, that he had been in mining there, zinc, but the veins had run dry, so Zack packed it all up, which wasn't much of a pack by that time, and came to Norman to work for a rig supply company. It was a new company, Zack told him, whose owner had a tip from a friend in Congress on a new field nearby, a huge basin, meaning a new boom for this part of the state. Zack winked at Bascom, who nodded slowly and put one finger to the side of his nose, acknowledging the secret and grateful for it. Zack told him that he was staying over at the Beeson place--which he actually was--and that he had found a place in the center of town, a clean little apartment right above a bank. "Should be safe," Zack said, touching his wallet. The landlord needed a couple of days to paint.

Zack felt safer now that his story had been set. Any suspicions that might attract to Zack would have to flow through Bascom, and they were now friends for life. Zack had originally thought to stay away from anyone in Norman, but the loner is culpable. Feeling safer, he decided to venture a certain line of questioning which might make his stay a little nicer.

"Listen, Bas," said Zack. He leaned forward and drew in the cook conspiratorially. Zack had been begged to call the man Bas.

"I don't suppose," he said looking around the room, then whispering into his coffee cup, "you know of anywhere around here where a man could get a drink of something stronger than coffee."

Bascom, who had drawn himself in, now drew away. Zack figured he had pushed too far, so he tried to cover himself. This was religious country, and Zack never knew when he would run up against someone whose decency he might offend, even in this part of town.

"I'm not much of a drinking man myself," Zack said. "But I've got this arthritis something terrible--the mines, you know, kept me out of the war--and the pain is sometimes too much. Ever since this Prohibition, it's gotten a bit difficult to ease the pain. What can an honest man do?"

Zack rubbed his hands, working out the pain. He was expecting either a lecture on the evils of drink--one got many such lectures--or a convoluted set of directions to a darkened alley with a hidden door and an involved password.

Instead, Bascom knelt behind the counter, rustling and clinking, and came up with a brown bag, which he set proudly on the counter.

"Normally this bottle costs three dollars," said Bascom, leaning against the counter, proud to be Zack's confidant. "But for you, it's only two. I like to help out a friend."

Zack plunked down four coins and peeked into the bag. Whiskey. Bascom swept the coins off the counter and dropped them neatly into his apron. Zack understood how Bascom's Diner thrived despite the lack of food being served.

"Hope that arthritis eases up," said Bascom, and both men laughed.

Zack shook Bascom's hand, grabbed his bottle and left. As he reached to the door, pushing it open with his behind, Bascom yelled to him to come back in the late afternoon, when he'd have another surprise for him, and he gave Zack a big wink. Zack figured what Bascom meant but was in too much of a hurry to give it much thought now, though he was certain he'd be interested later.

In the creaky hotel--*day wk month*, said the sign--Zack pulled the chair close to the window, where he sat with his legs propped on the bed. He rolled a cigarette and tucked it behind his ear, then rolled another cigarette. Zack opened the bottle and inhaled from it. The whiskey smelt of a dusky summer evening in Virginia, that air thick with humidity and peat. Zack placed the bottle between his knees and lit the cigarette, a long inhale and exhale, then he carefully brought the bottle to his lips and took a long draw from it. The drink warmed him, as if heat itself, flowing all the way into his tired boots.

He took three strong draws from the bottle, gasping for air after each one, then he set it down while he smoked and watched the street. He nursed the bottle after that. Immediately the liquor had gone to work, letting his brain click free and the thoughts flow again, undiluted by his circumstances. The world outside the window--dusty streets and ambling men, impoverished trees and derelict buildings--all seemed brighter to him, dimensional. Oklahoma, it happened, was capable of beauty.

He sat in the window the entire afternoon, smoking cigarette after cigarette and sipping from the bottle until half of it was gone. He drank rusty water from the hotel tap. He followed in his mind how he had got there, from marrying Eva and that initial sense of power to the drudgery of their lives and the continual need to move. Sitting in Norman, moving again or getting ready to, being away from Eva and the kids and the god awful plowing in the direct sun, he felt he could stay there forever in that slanted hotel room, staring out the window and eating at Bascom's. He would not return to his farm or his family. Let them get to California on their own.

But California. Always the last place, ever since he was a child, the old war still talked about in Virginia, California was the place they could always go to, and at some point it seemed to him as if California were the true eventual goal, the moving and the farming in between the requisite punishment for paradise. When Zack was a teenager in Virginia, his mother had lost two last children, both stillborn, and she had blamed it on the land's stinginess, as if it were contagious. She decided that California was the cure for her fragility. She had found--he could not fathom where she got it, not remembering any magazines in their house ever--and pinned to the wall of the kitchen near the sink a magazine article about the Edenic, health-giving properties of California. She had got everyone in the family, and many of the people at church, stirred up about California, thumping her kitchen table as a preacher might when demanding repentance. When they moved to Texas, his mother had known they were only going that far, having long conceded her dream. Still he had seen in his mother's dulled eyes the slow determination to continue on to California, if not for herself, then for the family and the families to come.

The magazine article carried a photograph of an orange grove in full fruit, the thick rows of trees marching off into infinity. For years Zack saw California through the distorted lens of that photograph. The article frayed and fell apart at the folds, but the picture continued fresh for him until after they moved to Texas, where he realized that California might not be anything like that photograph at all, except maybe that small part of California where that one orange grove bloomed eternally. California might turn out to be as impossible to furrow as any other field of wretched earth. It might all be an illusion, the way Texas had been. But somewhere in his prescient disillusionment with California, Zack had let fly into his head and stick there *gotta be better than here* and that was all that he needed to keep California from slipping out of his grasp because he knew that it had to be better than Texas and Oklahoma, and always *better than here, gotta be* because most days any place would have been better than where he stood over the plow with the impudent sun asking impossible questions. California had stayed in his head, not as the place it was, but as the next place. The last next place. Taking another sip of the surprisingly good whiskey, Zack pondered how California would differ from his idea of it, not if, but when he got there.

So that argument was over quickly: whether to leave his family or not. He always scrapped with that one when he drank, the liberation of his head extending to the desire to free his body from the boundaries of Eva or the children or the farm, but the family always won out, those obligations one and immutable. That argument over, then, having decided to stay with the family, he let himself ponder, for relief, the lovely thought of staying in the hotel window forever and forgetting he had a family.

Cigarettes and another quarter of the bottle, and the sun was already beginning to set, the jobless quarter of the town still quiet, unobliged to follow the come and go of the working districts. Zack could not see the sunset directly from his window, but watched instead the red and diffuse pinks of evening as they settled like dust on the buildings across the way. The buildings drew closer under the scrutiny of the dusk. *Sailor's delight.*

At the diner Bascom served up a real steak sautéed in onions, red and green peppers, garlic and lemon, and potatoes in herbs and butter. Zack cut open the steak with a ragged knife and saw that it was seashell pink with brown and red juices sopping in and around it, the juices flowing into the wall of potatoes that ringed the plate. Zack let the steak sit on his tongue, then he chewed a few times and swallowed the piece almost whole.

"Perfect," he said.

"Almost, but not yet," Bascom said.

Bascom set a coffee cup of red wine in front of Zack. The wine was thick and chewy, almost bitter. The next bite of the steak was that much better, as was then the next sip of the wine.

Zack, sated, tried to pay for the meal but Bascom would hear none of it again, shoving the tower of coins back across the counter. Finally Zack plunked down half of the coins far out of Bascom's immediate reach, an undeniable tip. Bascom ignored the money and cleaned up the plates. When he was finished, he stood before Zack who complimented him endlessly on the meal, reliving it in words for the both of them to savor. Bascom then motioned with his head to a far corner of the diner, and Zack swiveled on his stool.

It was full dark now, and the diner was crowded with strangers. At a corner table sat a woman who stared at Bascom and Zack. Zack nodded at her. She smiled, then came to the counter, setting herself in a dainty fashion on the stool next to Zack, letting Bascom take her hand as if she were entering a coach. She turned to Zack.

"Zachariah Oliver," Bascom announced quietly. "May I introduce Merrilee Smithson."

Zack reached up to tip his hat, but it rested on the stool next to him. He rose a few inches. When Bascom had used Oliver rather than Macoby when introducing Zack, it startled Zack only because the wrong name fit so well, as though he had already moved into his other life.

Merrilee was a few years younger than Eva, but she had not been a farmer's wife, Zack knew, because she had not been ravaged and shaped by the land the way Eva had been. Merrilee's skin was still smooth, like porcelain, her red hair had life to it, and her face, while it showed troubles of its own, was not haunted by the loss of children or the worries of the crops. Her own troubles, Zack imagined, rootlessness, drinking maybe, seemed minor pleasantries, small intrigues that gave her character but which had not robbed her of her fire yet. She was taller than Zack by several inches, slender, thin-boned, with bobbed hair. Her wide, thin lips were naturally painted-red red.

Zack offered to buy her a cup of coffee, which she accepted by dipping her head to one side. After he'd ordered the coffee, Zack pushed some crumpled bills across the counter and held up two fingers. Bascom retrieved two bottles wrapped in paper from the back room, then busied himself at the far end of the counter, his back turned.

"Where you from?" Zack asked, staring into his coffee.

She was from Hibbing, Minnesota, which Zack heard instantly when she drew out the word Minnesota. She had come to Norman because it was an oil town, wildcats and riggers passing through. The idea, she told him, had just got stuck in her head and she followed it. Bad ideas, she told him, seemed to get more easily stuck than good ones. When Merrilee spoke, she spoke out of the side of her mouth, not from timidity, but as if her words were too much for this world.

"Why don't we go back to your place and have a drink?" she said, folding her thin arms and drawing herself up on the counter. "It's a long story you've invited in. I'd like to tell it to you."

The invitation did not surprise Zack; he had encountered such boldness before on his *little trips*. Zack met women in speakeasies or in diners, and once in a church meeting in a town so dull that church was the only entertainment. Zack had been to a prostitute one time in his life, but the affairs he had on his trips were nothing like that. The time he had gone to a prostitute he had gone with his brothers on a spree after the one century-crop any of them would ever see. They rode to the next town, drinking in the wagon and howling through the still night. The bordello was a run-down hotel with an air to pretensions so ill-realized that the decorations could not even attain garishness.

His brothers clucked the whole time like chickens at feed, and mistaking Zack's silence for shyness rather than embarrassment, teased him mercilessly as each was led away to a different room by a different woman. Zack went through with it, but it was such a cold experience, so short and without smiles, it held for him none of the pleasures, the talking low and stroking, that being with a woman for real held. The woman he chose that night, more a girl really, all of Zack's age if not younger, was as businesslike as if she were filling out a will. Zack tried to talk to her, but she kept him on course and would have none of it. When he tried to talk to her after, she kicked him out, threatening to call the bouncer. Her face had been hardened by her contempt, and underneath that steely mask Zack saw her fear and rage, her dislike for everything that came into contact with her. Half the trip home, Zack driving the wagon, his brothers yipped and bayed, then finally gave way to vulgar snoring.

The women he met on his trips away from the farm were not prostitutes, though money did change hands. He had no illusions about these women, knowing that had he been insolvent they would have as likely not paid a whit of attention to him. But these matters had not been business, more pleasure. Times had been tough for everyone, especially for women living alone in cities, given that most of them had children. Some good food, some drink, some tobacco, a bag of groceries and a little money, all seemed fair trade for company, or so Zack believed, believing also that the women believed it. Each woman had stayed the night with him, and each time Zack had left the woman with a small pile of coins, as much as he could afford from his bounty. Prices were never argued. It was a struck deal, Zack knew, a silent bargain. It was not business.

He and Merrilee walked the lighted streets with the sounds of churches and speakeasies twisting in the humid night. Merrilee had come to Norman for the prostitution, to make her fortune. She had believed someone's story about the lucrative oil business and the money that the men were giving away just to keep it from drowning them, there was so much of it. Zack thought of his mother and her swallowed-whole tales of California, and of how his father believed more simply that the next forty acres over were the best forty acres anywhere, and he thought of himself, getting ready to go to California, and he laughed out loud for the troubles of everyone and how *we, all of us, every single god damn one* is ready to believe in the next county over. Merrilee stopped in the street and asked him what he was laughing about, and he told her and they both laughed, happy to be no longer alone in their illusions. Zack rolled cigarettes for them as they strolled in the night, content to wander through the noisy town. Zack moved to the other side of her, where he could watch her talk out of the side her quick, inviting mouth. She put her arm in his.

She had entered herself into a bordello the day she arrived in Norman. She was seventeen and as frightened as the day of the night, but she outlasted her fear, dreaming of ease and fortune. She hated every second at the bordello, but stayed for almost four years before she got fed up and left. She hadn't saved a penny, spending it all on liquor to get her through the next day and night. She got a job cutting fabric for rich ladies in the department store downtown. She hardly made any money doing that and still had to live in a rat hole, but it was easier to hate rich ladies than to hate all men. That was years ago. She still cut fabric, but was allowed to keep the scraps and made quilts from them, which she sold to her customers for extra money. She fancied that the rich ladies passed them off as their own handmade quilts.

Zack listened with his head down as they walked, taking in her words and the strange tones of her accents. Part of the great pleasure he derived from his excursions--he preferred to call them that--was meeting people like Merrilee who would tell you their stories, good, bad, or otherwise. On the share lands, in the little church villages there, everyone claimed to piety, even though it might be the furthest thing from the truth of their lives, pretending that their lives weren't really happening to them, pretending that they had already ascended. In the bigger towns, though, people with real lives were more than willing to share them with a stranger.

Merrilee asked about Zack. He hated to tell her the lies that he told to Bascom, and he tried to weave in as much of his real life as he could. He knew that Merrilee might as easily be lying to him as he was lying to her, but that didn't matter much. Both were happy, he believed, to be with each other, listening to good stories, true or otherwise.

In his barren hotel room Zack and Merrilee drank Bascom's whiskey. They turned off the overhead lamp and sat in the glow of the streetlight, smoking and talking, telling their darker stories, those reserved for unlighted night. When Merrilee told her most difficult stories, her eyes fluttered and closed, revealing only their slimmest crescents, and spoke, as she had all night, out of the side of her mouth. Her square jaw, her thin neck. Finally there was a narrow silence. Zack stared at her bright, coy mouth and contemplated staying in Norman forever, saying to himself *so that's about it*. Merrilee was tired of talking now--it fatigued her, that was obvious--and she rose from her place on the bed and moved to Zack and kissed him with her red tongue. They removed each other's clothes, standing in the near dark, Zack stroking her bony back over and over, amazed at the softness of her skin. Merrilee held Zack's hand and bit his wrist, then bit and licked her way up his arms to his neck, which she sucked softly, moving her tongue over it, until Zack shivered.

ZACK woke in the middle of the night, from the drinking. Brown liquors always did that to him, startling him awake after a few hours of dead sleep, but what kept him awake for the several hours after was the pain in his hands, the pain like sprung steel. The pain had first come to him when he was in his twenties, after the harvests, his hands slashed and bleeding, which damage was always there. One year, after a harvest which was neither particularly brutal nor large, the pain deepened, embedded in the muscles and tendons and bones themselves, a pain as much a part of his anatomy as his blood. Year after year the pain thickened, attacking him mostly at night, at random, without waiting for the harvest, exploding whenever it chose. He could do nothing for the pain but drink, which did nothing for his hands but made the long nights more tolerable. He massaged one pained hand with the other, the good of that in keeping the one hand busy and forgetting some of that hand's pain. In the beginning Eva used to wake also and massage his hands for him, as he would often, in the beginning, rub her feet for her when she was pregnant, but Eva was impossible to wake in the middle of the night any longer and Zack's hands hurt too much to soothe his wife's feet.

He sat on the edge of the bed, Merrilee twisting a bit in her fit sleep, and stared out the window at the nude, blue town. Here was his last chance, he knew. He might shake Merrilee awake right now, not a minute later, and strike some deal with her, beg her to join him in Norman, concoct for each other a brand new life, create something out of all the nothing that both of them possessed, leave all of himself behind and start fresh again. But he could not make the move to disturb her peacefulness and her soft snoring, and the moment passed, leaving only the shards in his hands. Eventually the pain dulled, though persistent, and he lay on the bed, rubbing his hands, waiting for the night to slice its way past him and leave him tired and washed in the gray dawn. He fell asleep thinking that he would never fall asleep again.

When he woke in the morning, Merrilee was gone, as he knew she would be, and gone also were the bills and coins he had left out for her. Had he been awake when she left he would have given her more.

He washed and went to Bascom's for breakfast, Bascom insinuating and questioning with his eyes but getting only the satisfaction of Zack's silence. Zack walked down the street and, with the last of his money, bought enough tobacco to get him home. *How quick*, he thought of the money, running the calculations and unable to track it all, *must some of it go for being alive and breathing the air.*

In the scraped hotel room, he drank and smoked and looked out the window and watched everyone else lead their lives, and he thought about what he would have to do the next day. In the evening he went for a walk and hoped, without whispering it to himself, that he might run into Merrilee.

Against his better wishes he wandered back to Bascom's, the diner thriving on coffee and paper bags on a Saturday night, and he sat at the counter and let Bascom make him up some chicken for which he refused payment, Zack knowing that would be the case, banking on it. He had come back partly to look for Merrilee--Bascom had not seen her--and partly because he had got hungry again. Two days of real meals, real food, had left him hungrier than years of nothing but greens and lard bread and fatback and molasses and sowbelly. The real food had started something up in him again. He said good night to Bascom but meant good-bye and went back to his hotel room and drank the last half of the last bottle and stared out the window and thought of nothing and finally fell to sleep. He was so tired, *years of tired*, that he slept through the pain in his hands, and when he woke up, it was time to get to the business.

ZACK washed up and smoked a cigarette, then he left the blank hotel room for the last time. Sunday morning had come thick and blue to Norman. All was quiet, the church bells an hour from their vain peals. Zack took to the back alleys, *where I belong anyway*, until he passed the downtown and began the incline to the big houses on the bluffs. Fat smoke from red chimneys stirred the sky.

He stopped outside one of the large houses, an older one with gables and turrets, and placed himself behind a crumbling portion of ivy-covered stone wall. He was hidden from the street by a large elm, from where he was able to see the garage and the front entrance of the house. On the other side of the wall a low maze of hedge zigzagged the yard, offering concealment. He waited for dogs to come at his scent, but either there were no dogs or they were at their meal, snuffling over their bowls, leftovers better than anything Zack's family ever ate except for maybe at Christmas and funerals. He waited for the longest time, his legs stiff from standing still.

A young man in livery came out of the kitchen and went to the garage to start the car. He walked as if he might be the owner of the car, and when he pulled the long silver car out of the garage to the front entrance, the young chauffeur leaned imperiously on the fender of the car with the arrogance of hired help.

From out of the house poured a room-sized blur of color and coats that drew itself into several components, a youngish couple and their three children, and a young blonde woman who must have been the maid or the nanny or a hapless relative invited to share in the wealth for a bit of attending and making the couple feel superior. The young woman fussed after the children, snapping their coats closed. Fur collars. Zack saw and felt the snap in the air and realized for the first time, so used to it in his thin black coat, that the season had drifted and spun in the last few days; hot days still, but chilling at night. The mother, high strung and snapping her gloves, came after the young woman and re-fixed everything. The father, stuffed into his starched shirt, unable to bend to his children, able hardly to look down at them so far away on the ground, stood by snapping his gloves, too, as though this were the code that held his family together. He lorded his position in his stance, although there seemed to be no threat to his domain. Assembled and appropriate, the family and its attendants stood quiet for one of those flash moments, then all was noise and blur again as they climbed into the long car and left the house empty.

Good, thought Zack, *perfect*. New money, boom money, oil money, money that would leave itself lying all over the house in piles that could easily be converted, not stashed away in old family things. Cash.

He made the window on the first floor, hidden by a scratching holly bush, and found it open and knew from this that these were foolish, heady people who believed that their money protected them from everything. They deserved to lose some of it, practically giving it away like this. What he took would not kill them, would not in the least interfere with the accumulation of more wealth, but it would be enough to make them sit up and take notice. He wanted that.

His boots touched plush carpet, his feet unaccustomed to that give, as though he had stepped into a swamp. The house was a hush. Empty, he knew, the instant he breathed it.

He wanted nothing more than to roam the high-ceilinged halls and rooms and to look at and touch everything, but he had business to attend to, and he had to ensure his business was in place first, so he headed up to the second floor in search of the master bedroom. Sunlight dropped in slants across the room, like curtains especially imported for this house and its perfect inhabitants.

The first time he had stolen --*I am a thief,* he whispered to himself that first time, over and over again until the words signified nothing--he had not known he was going to burglarize someone's home. His first attempt to raise the needed money, cardsharping, had failed; robbery was too intimate, too face to face. On the first of his *little trips*--her voice always with him--on another Sunday walking past an empty rich house in another faceless, dusty boom town, it had come to him how simple it would be, so he broke a window and went in and found in one pile all the money he needed to pay the share rent, which was late owing to the drought. And after that, in different towns, for different serious mandates that life and weather and circumstance and betrayal handed down to him, five more times, he found the money that he needed lying in the houses of the rich neighborhoods, the money like fallen fruit. He always found the money in the bedrooms, even the one time he found a safe and was forced to chop it out of the wall with an axe and beat the safe with the axe until the door sprung. The bedroom, where everything good and secret was kept.

He found the master bedroom and began the careful search, always careful if possible, but never afraid to use an axe or a stone or a gun, whatever was at hand. *I am a thief.* But careful first. He looked in the jewelry cases, regarding himself in the crystalline mirror. Looked in the drawers, first through the man's socks and underwear, and then through the woman's underwear, taking a whiff of her soft silk, then he found the purple velvet bag and felt the crush of bills there. It might take them ages to discover this money was gone, and then they would suspect the maid. He opened the bag and laid the money on the thick bed. Two thousand dollars. *Fools.* He took it all.

Zack wandered the top floor of the house, all the time in the world now, and peeked into a life that might as well have been life on the moon. A knot of craving bundled in his stomach, for a life he knew he would never own, a craving he hadn't had until that first time when he peeked into someone else's rich life and took their money away with him. Sometimes at night on the farm, his hands gnawing their way out of his skin and muscle, he used these empty, voluptuous rooms as his salve and ointment.

Ghostly, he thought, *I am a ghost.* He wandered the halls. Downstairs in the kitchen a bounty of leftover eggs and fresh-baked sweet rolls, a pot of hot coffee and a fire in the fireplace, which Zack prompted with the toe of his dusty boot. For the first time since leaving the farm, Zack thought of his family as something other than the thing to which he must return, the idea behind his coming here, thought of them as something other than the thing from which he was absent, the foundations of the toil which was the breath--inhale and exhale--of his everyday life. He thought of them as they must have been at that moment, in church like every poor soul in the world, on a quiet Sunday morning, Eva listening to the preacher, the children fidgety, kicking the bottoms of the pew, waiting for that moment of release when they might run around in the churchyard with the other children.

Nimion, his oldest, was that age where getting out of church was not for hunting or frog-gigging or scratching around in the dirt with the other boys, but a time for wondering where the girls in the congregation might be going after church and what they might be doing, and only the girls, having forgot entirely about boys at all. Elwell, the younger boy, was deaf to that roar yet and crushed by his brother's heresy. The girl, Mary Minerva, played with her doll, insensitive to it all, yet strangely preparing herself for it by playing with her one ragged doll. And of course, Zack thought of Eva, inevitably, for that's where these children came from, obvious yes, but as the fellow said, inevitable, because you could not look at her body, her face, any part of her, and even in Norman in a rich man's house, could not even think of her without seeing sharply the changes, damages mostly, that bringing those children and the two other dead children into the world had wracked upon her. And the same damages, maybe more, of caring for them and feeding and clothing them and trying to make them into something in her eyes despite their natural stubbornness and the predilection of the individual to be what it will be, must be. ˙Zack saw the damages the compromises brought to her face and body, the compromises between what she had wanted her children to be, and what they refused to be.

Eva, his wife, seated in church, in her one black calico dress, frayed now--he would buy her a new one, store new and not just a bolt of cloth. She prayed with crabbed hands clasped on a kerchief, her head bowed. She prayed so hard sometimes she cried. She prayed for their move, and the health of the children, and for rain, and redemption for the sinners of this world. Eva and Zack had always gone to church--it was the center of share life, the village square--but Zack realized that after years of breaking the fallow soil, after their move from Texas to Oklahoma had tricked them, that Eva not only went to church, she believed now, pulling away from him and drawing closer to God, depending on the strength of the assembled church, confiding in that body. She prayed all the time, swooned at meetings and accused Zack of godlessness. She was saved now, immersed in the water, saved as much for the salvation and eternal rewards and duty of it, thought Zack, as for being dunked in that tank of cool water that had been Zack's only temptation to salvation. Eva sat in church, praying for Zack and his safe return and his freedom from sin.

Zack stole packaged cigarettes and a small bottle of schnapps and left the rich man's house, replenished, joyous at his, Zack's, fortune. He walked back down into and through the town, his head bowed, hidden below his hat brim, and because it was Sunday and the virtuous were in church and the sinners still asleep, he walked alone and unnoticed to the train station.

The train left Norman after noon, pulling into the stupid sun, but something had changed in the insipid landscape. Now that Zack was leaving, the land itself seemed to give way, to let down its guard and expose its beauty. Or maybe any landscape was more beautiful when you rode in a seat and not in a boxcar, and when you had a wad of bills tucked under your arm. The sky was high, deep blue, streaked with tail feather clouds that stretched out as if jumping over Oklahoma, beautiful in their attempt to avoid rain. The dogwoods that rimmed the small bluffs on the outside of town gave up their leaves, which yellowed, shivered and turned in the breezy day.

He was leaving it. Any place passed through was a place to admire. The land, this land here, this stamped and untamable plot, drought-stricken and bordered by still more drought, was no longer his adversary, simply a piece of earth like every other piece of earth that didn't break your hands and back by resisting the plow. Even the desolate Oklahoma landscape, now winding out of the Norman bluffs and back into the flat, unimaginable plains, had its allure and beauty. The beauty was in the desolation. This was a land where Jesus might have wandered, broken and doubtful. On the train, the hum and chatter of the other passengers went unheeded by Zack as they shot through the solitude, for Zack was wrapped in that solitude. He was wrapped up in saying goodbye to the land that he had hated since the first day the wagon's wheels had crunched over its rutted roads. He was leaving it now; it was beautiful.

AT the top of the last summit, they stopped. Zack had been listening to the Model A's wheeze through the last several desert valleys, and each time the car rose choking to the top of the next hill, he hoped--asked Eva to pray--that it was the last hill. He could not hide his disappointment. He had known the stories of California were too good to be true, so he had toned down his pictures of that Eden, driven into him by his mother and her magazine article, and adjusted the green from jungle-bright to something less rain-soaked, eliminated half of the wildflowers and orange groves, limited the size of the streams and the trout that jumped in them. Still, his attempts to be realistic were grandiose compared to what he saw before him. He could not believe his bad luck. He had stolen for this, had packed up his family and moved them away from the bigger family, had torn them out of a land that, however harsh, was known. They had traveled through a scorching autumn, only to find this, another desert.

Eva comforted him by suggesting that the valley got richer as you moved farther north. But no, anyone could see. Flat, arid, and scrubby, California, he saw right off, had been a lie, simply the next place again, and not the last place as he had hoped.

They ate by the side of the road. The children ran in circles, Eva and Zack sat next to each other. He stared at the hazy horizon, trying to see what lay beyond it. In the November heat, the sun low against the sky, skidding across it, the long light filtered through the dust, the far side of the valley was invisible, the valley floor went on forever. Zack could see irrigated fields, shocks of green in perfect rectangles, but he had seen that scale of irrigation before and knew that it would never belong to a man like himself, never belong to one man unless that one owned hundreds of men. It would not be easier here.

They had worn their best clothes the entire trip, even though it had been too hot. *Sharecroppers*, Zack thought, *thinking we are going to be somebody else as soon as we cross a border, that just by letting some guard inspect our groceries at a gate in Arizona we will be passed on to a better life, in our finery.* He had shamed them, he saw now, by gathering them into the shade of his illusions. He had led them to believe that they could be different, Eva believing him for the first time in years, believing so much that they had dressed up like this, dressed up because he had given them both the new clothes and the belief required to fill out those new clothes.

They ate their lunch on the crest of the hill overlooking the longest valley in the world. Zack knew two things clearly. First, the children ought to enjoy the bread and the sardines and the fruit because there would not always be this for them to enjoy. The second thing tied irrevocably to the first because they both concerned disappointment, easing himself and the family into it, almost as if he himself had conceived of the disappointment and brought it on, the disappointment a good and inevitable idea.

Fuck you, was the second thing, playing like a harmony against the first thing. *Fuck you*, and he meant this land, this California, cursing it because it was barren and arid and, Zack could see from here, took too much effort to make it yield. He cursed it for being the same as the other land, perhaps all land. He could remember Virginia, when a boy, the green lush pastures and hills, and Lord, the rivers and lakes and creeks, rain in the summer, for god's sake. But there had not been enough of it there--land--and they were at the bottom, and so there was no question about whether to leave or not because at least there were shares available in Texas, then in Oklahoma, where there had been land and no water, and now here in California, no water either, at least not the kind you could get to unless you owned it. From the crest of the hill, Zack mapped the straight canals of owned water. *So, fuck you*, he thought, *fuck you for making me forget who I was and making me forget that there is no better place ahead, fuck you very much.*

Eva stopped asking questions, had stopped talking altogether, and instead busied herself with cleaning up the picnic that didn't really need cleaning up, after all, making work for herself as she was capable of doing when she avoided Zack. The disappointment hung between them as thick and unmoving as the haze that bolted shut the lid of the valley.

They drove into the valley, down winding hills covered with scrub oak, and when they reached the valley floor they drove on impossibly straight roads that followed the perfect canals, fields going off to the east and the west forever. The children fell to sleep; Eva was quiet and still. The day had started out hot and miserable, as the entire trip had been, but as they drove north, following signs to Modesto, the afternoon grew breezy and cloudy, and by dusk, had clouded over completely, cooler.

Eva located a patch of trees next to a canal, where there was a level place and no houses nearby. Zack fashioned a tent from a piece of canvas, and Eva made a fire, and the kids ran around one another taunting themselves with the dangers of the sleek, smooth canal. Eva cooked bread and chicken, but without herbs. After dinner, closing on dark, everyone had a small piece of chocolate, which was all the dessert anyone thought they deserved or needed, but Zack came back from a cigarette with two fists full of wild strawberries he'd found growing near the edge of the canal. The berries were sweet and bitter. Then, with the dark on them and the wind picking up, it began to rain, at first big splattering drops that left craters in the fine dust, then pelting, then a sheet, the first rain of the season. The smell of the dust rose from the rain, a land cloud, and the smell invaded his nose and his memory.

Fuck you again, he thought, crouched under the canvas, still referring to the land. He thought two things again. This time *fuck you* was the first, unforgiving of the land. He cursed the land for its double cross, tempting him as it did with its strawberries and little bit of rain. *One rain and you forget everything.* He cursed the land as far as might be seen on a clear day, cursing it to Modesto and beyond--the longest valley--cursing it because he knew this land would give him just enough to get him started and keep him going, but never enough to be happy. A little rain and everyone would be convinced they could make it here, one sweet mouthful of strawberry and they would kill themselves trying to make it work. If California was not going to be Eden, lush, dripping, water fallen Eden, then it should have been the Sahara and let everybody pass it by instead of seducing them with the perfume of a little rain.

Fuck you, then, was the first thing, right in the front of his head, playing at his lips as if he might get down on his hands and knees and yell at the land and pound on it with his fists. What was in the back of his brain, the second thing, was the most ironic and dangerous thought of all, *maybe I can make it here.* Despite himself, despite his curses, this second thing occurred to him and slowly weaved through him. Sometimes, at a gathering, someone will hum a song that someone else does not particularly like, and the person humming it will be far away in another corner of the gathering--a wedding, a funeral--but not so far that the tune cannot be heard. Then the person who does not like the song, not really having heard it, would never have reported to anyone that the song had been heard, suddenly starts to hum that song on the way home from the gathering. That person then realizes that they're humming the song, then tries to chase the hated song from the world by humming another song, but the first song, tenacious, sticks in the mind and follows for days, maybe even weeks. That was the second thing; it would nag at Zack for weeks to come. *You could make it here*, the land hummed through the rain's teeth. *Make the land give way.* And each time the thought came up, Zack would curse it again. *Fuck you*, atavistically, hopelessly. Zack knew better.

The canvas held tight, and the plot where Zack had pitched the tent on bent willow branches was high enough to stay dry, so that the evening turned perfect on them, and he was unable to summon the requisite rage for chasing away his thoughts. The children fell asleep right away. Nimion snored the deeper snore of a boy in puberty, and Zack knew he could put him to work soon, and maybe with the two of them they could make the land yield, and maybe the younger boy, too. The rain, tapping on the canvas, gathered the family. Mary Minerva, blonde hair and skewed smile, slept between Zack and Eva.

Eva propped herself on one elbow facing Zack. He knew, had felt it coming, that it was time to talk. When they had first courted and married, Zack and Eva had talked long into the night, while lying in bed, or while courting, in the hayloft in the barn, but that fire to talk had been tamped out by the hardships they faced together. The silence had stayed tough with Zack and Eva over the years, broken only when the world's snapping weight on them was too much to bear alone. When the silence was broken, it was broken with strategy, not concern. Tonight, however, lying in the rain with his family, the irresistible song of hope humming away, the words came smoothly.

She smiled at him, and he began.

"Your cousins think we'll get of a place of our own at first?" he asked.

"What they said in their last letter," she said, looking off into the rain, the rain slowing, the canal rush thickening. "Was that we could easy get picking jobs right away, fruit or cotton, and that if we had enough to put down we could get a small place and scratch that way. But there ain't any shares here. We can stay with them--they got a place in town--until we get settled. We can live on the farms in little houses that the owners built--they all have electricity-- or we can get a place in town because now we have the car. The say the money is good, and someone with experience can become a foreman in no time. Lord willing."

Her words registered, but it was the rhythm of them he liked and that reverie he fell into, closing his eyes and listening to her talk. *It's the rain.*

"I think we start working right away," he said. "Picking. Put Nimion to work, too. Save the rest of the money, then look for our own place."

"The boy doesn't work," she said. "He stays in school. We live in town, if we pick. I won't live in a camp."

"You're right," he said. "We'll stay with your cousins, then. Find jobs, find a place. Take our time. I think we can do it this time."

"You're right," she said. "I think this place will be good."

It's the rain. Even though it was November, short-dayed and raining, the night was still balmy, the ground warm. If it ever rained again in Oklahoma, it would be cold when it did so. Maybe the land would give this time. *Maybe, but fuck you just in case.*

Eva talked, the wall breached for the moment, of her cousins and the church in Modesto. She dreamed a house for the family, small and cozy, painted white, bougainvillea overwhelming the porch. The porch, sitting at night, at least if it wasn't going to rain, there would be a porch to sit on and be cool, drinking tea. Electricity, she told him again, everybody had electricity. He told her of the houses he'd seen in Norman, but he did not tell her how he had come to know of them.

The fire came back to her eyes when she dreamed their house for them, and when Zack told her of the mansions, he saw the fire intensify. He reached across Mary Minerva in her tangled slumber and touched Eva's hand. She grabbed his hand and reassured him, but refused him.

"We'll get a nice little place," she said, and the fire flickered out.

They slept, warm in one another, the family huddle. Zack was spared the midnight visitation of the sprung steel in his hands; since he had left for Norman, he had not touched the handle of a plow or shovel or pitchfork. Sometime before dawn, he woke to a brief spurt of rain, light, almost a drizzle, and he knew that he had been right when he realized that this land would fool him with just enough rain to keep him hopeful. So he bound up his resistance to that hope in a tight ball of string which he clutched against his stomach, folding around it protectively, and slept again.

IN the morning, after coffee and bread for everyone, and the very last of the packaged cigarettes for Zack, they climbed into the damp car and drove straight on and up into California towards Modesto, driving deeper into the valley, the mountains on either side visible now from the clearing rain and the continued cloud cover. They drove into a landscape that was every mile more cultivated than the last, the crops changing by section, first cotton, then grains, and as they approached Modesto, nuts and fruits, as if, Zack thought, they could keep driving north and find a place where gold actually did grow on trees. Even Mary Minerva knelt on the seat, only four and incredulous, so obvious the plenty. They stopped at a roadside fruit stand and carefully chose pieces for themselves, one piece for each, and each piece split five ways, thrifty in their choosing, not for the money of it, there was still a lot of money, but as a resistance to how much of it there was. If they were to begin to indulge, they seemed to say to each other, Zack and Eva cautious in each other's gaze, the indulgence would multiply and bury them. They were cautious the way children are, wary, when offered an overflowing handful of candy. They ate the peach, pear, plum, apricot and orange, each fruit sweeter than the last, the sweetness of each combining with the others until their mouths were joyous and sticky. They left themselves craving more. The breeze blew cool but not cold through the open windows of the car.

       Fuck you once again, he thought. *We will never, not once, have that land. That argument is over. At least that is one less thing to think about. So, fuck you*, he cursed again, as they drove into the heart of the valley. He cursed continually, even as they drove into Modesto under the brand new lighted sign that arched over the main street, *Water Wealth Contentment Health*, and when they stayed with the cousins, pitching a tent in the backyard. He continued to curse the land when it provided jobs for them, him and Eva, and schools for the children, and he even cursed the land when it gave him a house, and he and Eva went down to the bank and signed papers on a note that promised the house would be theirs, and even the land it was built on, but that wasn't owning land, a house was just a house. He cursed the land again when they moved into the house, each of them sleeping in their own rooms, and electric lights, and a stove, and he cursed the land when the crops began to spring up in the backyard garden because it was actually raining and even if it didn't rain the people in the valley who owned the water apparently had enough of it to let Zack have what spilled over the tops of their teacups. He cursed hard because they ate better than they ever had. The land suckered them in. He cursed the land the whole time the land provided for him because he knew, had known the minute he saw the desolate valley, that the land would somehow take it all away and was lying in wait for him and his only vigil and protection was to say *fuck you* over and over again. He cursed because when the worst happened he could pretend to himself that he had known better. The sucker punch came in May of 1932, when everything looked good, after the last of the impossibly long spring rains.

MODESTO, a prosperous valley town at a confluence

of rivers, is the heart of the valley, halfway between San Francisco and Los Angeles and close enough to Sacramento for the lawyers and corporations there to keep an eye on it. When Zack moved to Modesto proper, it was a middleman's town of white houses and churches and shady streets and lots of automobiles. The migrant workers, the people who actually stooped to the work, lived on corporate farms behind barbed wire or on the outskirts of the town, like Zack and Eva in the quarter reserved for the likes of them and the Mexicans and the few Negroes and the sequestered Japanese fruiters.

       What came with such a protected and protective town, the middleman's community, was an overwhelming and stifling sense of propriety. The middlemen were humorless to the largest degree, as though to laugh or drink or pleasure in any way would let loose demons that might raze the town. Their piety kept them in control. Zack had expected, had heard rumored, that California was the new place, where tradition had yet to step in and strangle any vitality, but the same white men with their church-going faces ruled here, banning alcohol and dancing and brothels, a small enough town to be provincial and a big enough town to crush the foreign.

It was impossible to find a drink in Modesto. Eva's cousins were Bible thumpers, and the sermons Zack endured in their cramped, noisy church promised not, as he expected they would, eternal freedom of the soul, but an opportunity, veiled in religious phrases, for even the poorest to become as fat and rich as the middlemen of the white-housed town and their ruffled, Sunday families. People prayed to God that He might lift the burden of their mortgages. Zack spurned both the middlemen and their sycophants and the manner in which they spurned him, vehemently and without compassion. He held his family to their side of town and would not let them mix with other than poor children. Eva visited with her cousins on Sundays, when they all went off to church, but Zack stayed home after a few weeks of hypocritical sermons, cursing everyone in their churches. One day, he beat Elwell for playing with the daughter of one of the middlemen, hitting him on the bottom with a strap, offering no explanation.

Zack began to leave the house after dinner, excusing himself for a smoke. He wandered the poor side of town in the still and warm May air. A scent of citrus hovered over the town on these long evenings, sharp and particular.

Eventually, he found what he was looking for in the Negro quarter. One orange-soaked night he wandered past a man seated on the stoop of a boarded-up store, a bottle hidden behind the man's leg. The man, in deference, looked down and away from Mac, and the man said with bowed head "evenin', suh," actually that, to Zack's amazement, actually "evenin', suh," as if this were Virginia or Oklahoma or Texas, as if Zack were a rich white man. Zack almost said, wanted to say for the fun of it, *sholy ain't hit a fine evenin', boy*, all of it in mimicry, noting the other man's misery and hoping to get a laugh out of him, but Zack remembered the circumstances--solitary pitch night--and did not want to scare him. There was something else he wanted.

"Evenin'," he said, letting the accent out a bit, letting the man know of their shared past.

"Evenin'," Zack said and not wasting time. "I'd give you a quarter for a long swig of that bottle because I'm dead for it in this dry and priggish town."

The man offered the bottle freely. He had a funny, pinched nose and ears that were bent on themselves, his hair was dusted with cinnamon, Zack saw even in the moonlight. He looked up at Zack with a clear and calm expression, testing the waters, then smiled when Zack reached for the bottle.

"Any man who needs a drink bad enough to ask a nigger for it can certainly have one because I'm a Christian man, if still a nigger, and would not, daresay, could not, be cruel enough to deprive you."

The man's voice was free of the bonds and slurs which had held it before.

Zack took a long, two-gulp swig off the bottle, his eyes closed. It was pure corn liquor and burned his throat and brought tears to his eyes. The man on the ground reached up his right hand, and Zack immediately handed the bottle back, but the man waved off the bottle and held his hand flat.

"John Carver Ricks," he said, shaking Zack's hand. "But they call me Collie, for my ears, cauliflower,"

"Zachariah Taylor Macoby," he said. "They call me Zack because they haven't thought of anything else yet. Collie, it's a pleasure to meet you. I am, and will be forever, in your debt."

Zack raised the bottle in toast and again tried to return it, but Collie refused, and Zack took another long swig.

"Have a seat, Zack," Collie said, patting the cracked wooden stoop. "Looks like we've both found the friend we've been looking for."

"You can say that," said Zack. "I've been looking around this town since I got here, and I've found a lot of folks who will talk to you about taking a drink--why you shouldn't take a drink--"

"Ain't that right," chimed Collie.

"--but I have yet to find a decent enough human being to give you a drink. Too much talk about it and not enough drinking is what I say."

Collie handed him the bottle. The liquor no longer burned going down, instead its heat dissipated throughout Zack's body.

"Yes, indeed, Zack, yes, indeed." Collie clapped him on the back. "I have lived in this beautiful little town for three years now, and I have heard nothing from anyone except what they will tell you about what you should not do. Even in Niggertown. I'm telling you, it's a shame."

Zack rolled two cigarettes, lit them both and handed one to Collie. The moon was coming up over dusty orchards and sleepy houses. Far away a freight train pulled laboriously out of its yard.

"Zack, I like you," Collie said. "You are a generous man and you do not hold me against myself."

"Collie," he said, feeling the full weight of the liquor pressing against his brain. "What use is there in that? You are a man sitting on a stoop late at night, and it's too dark and too late and we are both too tired from working in the too hot sun for a man that is too white for either of us to know or care what color the other one is. I have a smoke, and you have a drink, and we both have a misery to share. So, we better share with each other because I don't see any one else around."

"And I imagine we both," said Collie, "have wives that are too churchy to let us relax too much."

They both laughed, then sat quiet for a moment.

"Collie," Zack asked. "Will you please show me where I can get some of this superb-nous corn liquor. I have got some money saved from where my wife doesn't know and ain't none of her business anyway, and I would love to get my tongue around some more of this juice, and I'd like to buy you some for yourself for a present."

Collie laughed and stood and stretched. He handed Zack the short bottle. Zack took a swig, Collie took the last swig and tossed the bottle, moon-gleamed, arcing high into the air and across the street into an orchard where it didn't break.

"Zack, my friend. We are going to Le Shaque D'Amour, if you truly do have money and are going to be the friend you seem to be."

"Believe what you see, Collie," he said, clapping him on the shoulder. "Always believe what you see, unless you know better."

Zack pulled several crumpled bills from his pocket. He had been wearing the bills smooth in his pocket for weeks.

Collie led him away from town through the poor section down a dusty, unpaved road. The half moon had risen puny.

Zack asked, so Collie told him as they walked along. Collie had come from Mississippi. Collie could not help himself when he said it and said *Missippi*, giving into the native tongue's pull. Zack noticed that his own language reverted in Collie's presence and was suddenly full of *ain'ts*, and his *it's* became *hit's*. Since coming to California, Zack had tried to rid himself of his native tongue, for anonymity.

Collie had been recruited by some agents for the California farms. The agents were going from small town to small town in Mississippi, telling the sharecroppers there of the opportunities in California. The agents spoke of the land's health and beauty, the incredible weather. Collie had known, he told Zack, that life here was not going to be as rosy as was painted for him, especially because they would be pickers and not farmers, but Collie heard that California was more tolerant of Negroes, that the terrible past had not happened there. Collie had never heard one story about the Civil War that mentioned California. So Collie and May and their two teenaged boys moved. They rode the train, the highlight of their lives. Collie financed the trip through various means, if Zack knew what he meant.

When they got to California they walked from Sacramento to Modesto where they were told fruit farmers were hiring. They lived at first in a company cabin, but conditions there were so unclean and brutal, the worst Collie had ever seen, that they finally moved to Niggertown. Collie's wife had been raped by company guards one night. It had almost killed them both, and they wanted to go back to Mississippi, but there was no money. Collie had never heard of anyone being lynched in California, but he suspected that that was only because he wasn't listening hard enough. Life was the same here as in Mississippi, narrow, constricted, almost impossible. But the weather was better; they didn't freeze in winter. Still, Collie had met a few white men, like Zack, that were different than the others. All those who had come to California running from the past were running from the same past. For whatever reasons they left the past behind, they were leaving it behind. Sometimes there was sharing in that exodus, shared relief.

Zack told Collie his story, including everything about Norman and the big house there. The dust rose in clouds around them as they trudged the orchard road in the quiet half-moonlight.

After some silence, smoking and walking, Collie spoke, as if from the middle of the quiet night.

"I bet it's like this walking on the moon," he said.

"I bet it's like this walking on the bottom of the ocean," Zack said.

Minutes later, in silence, they approached a small, slanted wooden house, set back from the orchard road. The house had a tin roof, rusted. Dull orange light glowed in the windows. Tinny scratches and deep laughs scattered around the house. A door slammed on the far side, and Zack heard slurred footsteps scraping off into the orchard. Collie stopped and waved his hand in front of the house, presenting it to Zack, as if he, Collie, had built and supplied it especially for his friend.

"Mr. Macoby," he said. "May I present to you, for your entertainment purposes, and for the general edification of your soul, Le Shaque D'Amour."

Zack bowed in accepting.

"Now, listen," said Collie, drawing Zack closer, breathing into his neck, co-conspirators. "It is most very likely that you will be the only white man in this place, and it is most very extremely likely that it, being your entrance, will cause a minor, if unspoken, commotion. But you are my friend, and you are with me, and in a little while, they will forgive you for being white. But they will never forget."

Zack nodded and followed. Collie knocked on the door with an especial rhythm, using both hands to tap out what Zack took for the entrance code. The door was opened by a man the very width of the door itself, the man having to bend down to peer out of the door. The man looked out from hooded, white eyes, and his stony glare made him impervious to inspection. He looked up and down Zack and Collie as if they were horses at auction and as if he would never bid on them. Collie thumbed over his shoulder to Zack, and the man let them pass.

The house was a one-room shack with the possibility of another room behind a swinging kitchen door that swung so frequently it seemed mechanized. The big room was filled with crowded tables, people standing around them where they couldn't sit. In the corner a gramophone blared tinny trumpets and slashed guitars and a dancing beat, the vocals deep and thorny. The entire room--the people and the chairs and tables, and the covered orange and blue lamps--all of it seemed to sway and dip to the music. Everyone was drinking and breathing long static clouds of smoke. Zack was parched.

Collie had been right; Zack was the only white man in the place. The room stiffened in little waves as people noticed Zack and Collie. The music grew louder in the gaps of the stopped chatter and filled the room's quiet places. Collie looked around for an empty table, scanning the room and moving forward into it. The chatter started up again slowly, water leaking from a rusted bucket.

"Collie," a soft voice said. "There's room over here."

Zack and Collie moved to a table in the corner near the swinging door. Collie introduced Zack to a young couple, who cradled drinks and seemed intent on each other, but they graciously spared Zack the time to look up, hear his name, shake his hand, and smile at him before returning to their intimate feast.

"I told you it would be all right," said Collie, raising his one finger at someone standing nearby, who then proceeded to disappear through the swinging door.

Zack looked around the room at all the faces there. There was something different about this speakeasy, different from any saloon Zack had ever known. The women here were not part of the entertainment, were not for sale or rented company. Zack could see that the women here were wives and girlfriends and sisters, and they were here as part of the gathering, not an addition to it. There were even a couple of tables where women sat together in groups, drinking and smoking, with no men present at all. Zack had never seen this among white people. Everyone was dressed to the nines.

A skeletal man in a linen suit placed a bottle of whiskey and two large glasses on the table. Collie attempted feebly to pay for it, but Zack was quick and forceful about his guestly duties. Zack rolled cigarettes, Collie poured drinks. Zack left the tobacco on the table and waved it to the couple there with them. They smiled and obliged. All four at the table clinked their glasses in a silent toast.

Zack had not spent a lot of time with Negroes, yet when he had dealings with them he had always felt that, contrary to the virulent opinions of his brothers and father, he had more in common with them than there were differences with which to feel superior. Both races were poor and worked for rich men who kept them poor. Both had families to support, families that were their burdens, cutting them the way a harness cuts a mule. Zack had known that the Negroes had other fears, which he was incapable of understanding, but were palpable nonetheless.

The first time he talked to a Negro, just talked with no business and no one else around, Zack registered the man's fear immediately. This was in Texas. Zack and the Negro, Raymond, sat together on the porch of the general store in Frogcreek Bend, waiting for supplies that had been ordered from Brownsville. Zack had been left at the store by his brothers hours before, and he was bored. The man who ran the store, a boy really, had nothing to say. Zack offered Raymond a cigarette. Raymond was a little taller than Zack, but chubby. Raymond had a pleasant face, cheerful it seemed in the pus-colored sun. When Zack offered him the cigarette, Raymond's face clouded and became impregnable. Zack held the cigarette out to him, his hand and gaze steady, saying nothing. Raymond slowly reached out for the cigarette, and cowering the way a stray dog will for a biscuit, snatched the cigarette from Zack's hand. Zack held a lit match, to which Raymond drew a little more boldly.

"Much obliged, sir," Raymond said, puffing on the cigarette. "I reckon you're waiting on Brownsville, too."

"You're welcome, sir," said Zack, lighting his own cigarette. "Indeed, I am. Waiting here in the same stupid sun as you, only you have your wagon and can go right away. I have to wait for my boneheaded brothers. I think you've got the better deal."

"Maybe," Raymond said, smiling now, revealing his pleasant face again, his true face. "Maybe."

Zack had always known that his people's hatred for the Negro race ran deep, embedded in almost everyone he had ever known. His brothers had nearly kicked a teenaged Negro boy to death one time, the beating conducted and orchestrated by his father. The beating had materialized out of thin air, centered on no immediate confrontation, the conflict an older one, a bloodier one, a conflict that seemed to have nothing to do with the members of this particular beating. The teenager had been walking alone in the middle of a Sunday, far out on a lonely road, obviously on some errand, for he walked fast. Zack, his brothers and father had left a church dinner to pick up some leftover roofing from a neighbor. Always so neighborly within their own. His father and brothers taunted the boy as they passed him, asking in singsong voices where he might be going on his momma's business.

The boy did not answer and mistakenly threw his chin out in defiance. Zack's father slowed the wagon, and the brothers got out, three of them, and poked at the boy until the boy swatted back. Then they were on him, and he was on the ground, and they were kicking him, and Zack's father stood in the wagon and yelled encouragements. It didn't take long before the boy was unconscious, or seeming so, taking one last boot to the stomach. They drove on, his brothers cackling like a bunch of hens. Zack, sickened and ashamed in the back of the wagon, was snubbed by his brothers and chastised by his father, *just a nigger boy*, he had said. Zack had not interceded on the boy's behalf because he knew that his heresy would have increased the duration and vehemence and awful sound of the beating.

Sitting in the orange and blue, music-filled room with Collie, drinking a passable whiskey, Zack wondered why the hatred had passed him over. Perhaps it was as with the land; the land had beaten itself out of Zack, had overlooked him because it had been beaten out of Zack's forbearers because they had beaten it out of the land. It had been too long and arduous a struggle for the race hatred to last forever, and Zack felt he was the end of it, the last straggling survivor of a battle so long no one alive remembered the original causes. Zack, warmed by the liquor and the crowded comfort of the room, had come at the end of the long line of hatred, the hatred, he hoped, beaten out of him, his body incapable of holding it.

Zack and Collie talked for hours, drinking and smoking. They talked about their lives from the bottom of their glasses and the bottom of the night. They told each other what they had never told anybody else, and although that was what he always told someone he drank with, Zack meant it this time. There was something about the equality of their situation and about Collie's willingness to listen and to talk back that made Zack more comfortable with Collie than with any other man he had met.

"That's bullshit, Zack," said Collie, pointing a finger at him. "It's not your wife's fault and you know that. She is just like you and she had everybody and everything pushing her around and telling her what to do, and making her do what they tell her to do. She's just like you, don't forget that. She suffers just like you do."

Zack knew that Collie was right, correct in everything he said that night. They drank until the bottle was gone. The speakeasy was still hopping, but Zack had to leave. Collie stayed behind to talk with other friends. Zack walked home through the dusty night orchards, the half-moon half through the sky and lighting the trees blue, silver, and white. The refrain, gone now for months, lulled quiet by the ease of life here, whispered again to Zack, from Zack, and he was surprised to hear it. *Fuck you*, he whispered to himself, *and keep fucking you* and this time he whispered it not only to the land, the fragile promises of the land, but to everything, the people and the land and all that transpired between.

ZACK and Collie went out almost every night. Sometimes they went to the blue and orange house, and sometimes they bought corn liquor and walked out of town along the river, where they fished by firelight with the other night fishermen, the riverbanks dotted with orange patches of wavering light. Once Zack and Collie hitched a ride up to Stockton and went to a Negro brothel, where Collie disappeared for half an hour, and although egged on by Collie and encouraged by the svelte madam, Zack stayed in the bar and talked instead, refusing not from the color of his skin, but because he did not like brothels. The two hitched back to Modesto, arriving at dawn.

Zack was no longer home. Eva was busy with the children or working in the fields. She sewed and cooked and washed continually. She was worn out, Zack could see, but he found himself incapable of stepping in to help, despite Eva's silent pleas. Nimion was getting out of control, staying out to all hours of the night. Zack beat him once before going out to see Collie, but that didn't seem to help. Eva never asked Zack where he was going, and she never demanded that he stay home. Zack figured it was because he paid for the liquor with his own money. Once the drink began to deplete the family paycheck, Zack would be in for a serious battle. Eva would not allow that.

Zack and Collie sat on the riverbank and talked about their lives. Collie lectured Zack on his responsibility to his family and his wife, and even though Zack reminded him that he, Collie, also had a family and a wife to which he was beholden, he, Zack, was told he ought to stay home sometimes and take care of business.

The family exhausted him. He had got them here, had worked too many years in the dead earth, had lifted his tired body too many mornings and endured the shards in his hands. He sensed that somewhere in the back of his mind, or his heart or his soul, wherever it was, somewhere in some small corner of his being, he wanted to give more to his family, but the fatigue of his life, the residual fatigue of the lives of his family and the families before that, kept him walled off from the desire to help any longer. He had done all he could do in his generation. He had got them to California, completed the crossing of the continent which had taken three generations. California was not paradise, to be sure, but he no longer believed in paradise. Eden was elsewhere, but his family would survive here. He would let his sons hike the next rung. It would not be Nimion who would do it, but maybe Elwell. Nimion was too wild; Zack had seen that right away, at just a few months old. Elwell was quiet and steady, also from the start; maybe Elwell would make the climb. Zack, almost fifty now, tired, wanted to be alone, had wanted that ever since he and Eva had stopped talking, knowing as he did that such a goodness, their time on the beach in Texas, could only last two days, never a lifetime. A lifetime was too long for anything.

And that phrase, his curse, haunting him again, filling him with foreboding. His whispered curse, an answer to the whispers he heard around him, the whispers he heard from the other pickers and from the bosses and the people in town. He had to, was forced to, as if held down at the neck with a crowbar, was made to answer their obscenities with his own, and so *fuck you* he whispered daily and hourly, for he knew a time was coming when the obscenities would come as close and tough as fists.

IT was the beginning of June, and the first of the hot nights had descended, covering the valley with a cloak. Le Shaque D'Amour was jumping that night, jammed to the quaking rafters, beating time. The windows and doors were opened, though that strategy provided no breeze in the crushed-to-death air. They had heard the party from a long way off and turned to each with voracious grins. There was something in the heat, Zack figured, that drove the house to such extremes, something about this heat being the first heat of the summer, an endless summer, hot without rain until October. They drank that night as if the liquor were cold water.

Collie and Zack stayed until long after the crush had departed. It was two in the morning. They talked about the home country, the south, talked about the bad food they missed and how wet the place was, lush and rotting. Zack told Collie of a bear hunt he had been on as a child, in the Blue Ridge-- when without any warning, Zack still thinking until the last minute that Collie was listening with his full heart, Collie very patiently arranged himself from seated at the table to lying on the floor, half curled around the table's pedestal. Zack toed Collie with his boot.

Zack left him there, determined to get home himself, not just for the soft bed of it, or the hot night walking home and the full, lighted moonscape, but also because, ever since their trip to the Stockton brothel, Zack had promised Eva he would always be home and in bed by dawn.

He expected the walk would cool him down, but even now at this hour, the heat would not give way. He wiped the sweat from his brow as if it were midday in Oklahoma and he was tethered to the damn mules.

When he saw the pickup truck of men in white shirts that glowed in the full beam of the moon, Zack wondered what they were doing out so late, respectable town middlemen such as these. They whooped and hollered and waved their hats at him as they drove past, and he waved back at them. The heat must have kept the whole town awake.

Zack wandered his straight course, loving for the moment the tight feel of the night, but that feeling dissipated, and he actually chilled the minute he saw the headlights coming at him, and not needing to know any more than the clench in his muscles, knew that it was the same truck that had passed him a minute before. The driver did not shift and rode the second gear too high. Zack knew more certainly than he knew that the moon was full and falling that the truck had turned around and come back for him, and he was whispering *fuck you, I knew it, fuck you again and endlessly.*

He arranged his best composure, his finest Sunday nonchalance, but the simple act of donning it revealed his fear. Only a dead man would not be frightened on this road with this truck load of tanked-up townies. Zack put his rudder face forward, walked up the road past them. The truck turned slowly around in the lane, then came even with him. The men in the bed of the truck stood.

"Evenin'," one of them drawled, his voice tipping towards Zack.

Then the other half of the greeting, delivered with more force, but still whispered, the word he had heard whispered all about him, one of the obscenities that had up until now only been a dreamed sound.

"Okie," the word like a brick tossed at his head, scarcely missing and thudding in the dirt.

Zack said nothing. The truck kept even with his brazen pace.

"Well, well," that hushed voice again, though not directed at Zack but at the others in the truck. Zack was incapable of looking up to see who spoke.

"It seems," said the hushed, growling voice, "that not only do we have us a dumb Okie here, we got one that is so dumb, it don't even understand God's English. Maybe it's truly dumb, as in deaf."

The laughter was followed by a single yelp, then a sailing sound followed by breaking glass.

"Hey, Okie," the voice yelled, chasing Zack to earth. "I said evenin', or didn't you hear me."

Then there was the pause, that gulp of air, the moment of understanding, then the air was sucked away and expelled again, and with that expiration came the second obscenity, the one heard constantly and not just in whispers, but this time the obscenity was paired with a second word, and combined with that second word, quadrupled in its force, implicating everyone in the world.

"Nigger-lover!"

As though that were the shamanic word, the one word that released all beastly spirits, there was a sudden great whooping and hollering from the truck, and the air filled with a great storm of obscenities, all of them aimed at Zack, who was puny in the dusty orchard lane. Zack ignored this dream and prayed for dawn, four hours away.

They were out of the truck, and the dream was inescapable. Perhaps this was Collie's dream, dreamed from under the table, and Zack had been caught up in it. The men surrounded him, dancing as it were, as Zack tried to walk himself awake. The truck screeched in the gravel, stopping short, and Zack knew it was over. He heard nothing, though words like arrows flew around him. He continued to walk, but that way was now impeded by chests and forearms.

"I said good evening, god damn, Okie, fucking nigger-lover," from the bulging face that captured Zack's vision. "I said good evening, you stupid bastard. Now what do you say?"

And knowing it was a mistake because it would forestall nothing, knowing the inevitable had begun long ago, in Oklahoma when he had decided to come here, even before that, a time no one alive could remember, knowing it would change nothing except that it would rob him of his dignity, rob him of his one refusal, but giving into it because he was suddenly tired and wanted nothing else but to lie down in the gravel, he said it.

"Good evening, sir."

"Oh, no, it's not," and the fist was already inside and through him, the men were on him.

And he knew then, the board cracking across his back, that he was gone, knew in that instant that it was over, his journey ended, knew that the family would be better off without him because even these men, these vicious stupid men, would not hurt his wife and his children, would probably in the end feel sorry for them and help them through their Christian charities if things ever got that bad for Eva and the children. And as the blows rained down on him, he gave up right there and let the fists and boot-toes dig into and carve out his flesh, resisting nothing, glad to be getting this over because he could not feel a thing any longer, because he was gone. The only sensation he retained in the flurry of bodies was in his hands, as if the whole wash of pain that flowed over him had been condensed into his hands; the crunch of the steel shards in his hands, snapping now, tearing into the muscle and trying to fly free from the flesh, was the only pain he felt.

They beat him to the ground and still beat him, and the intense pain in his hands was only a reminder that he was gone, that this life was behind him, that he would never have to live this moment again. The past that had led him to this spot was erased forever, erasing both the past from his body, kicked out of him, and erasing himself from that past, his body disappeared from that past, without a trace.

The beating stopped, and the men were back on the truck, screeching away. Zack lay on the ground, his only thought now was that the dust from the plume of the truck's leaving would settle back to earth and form a fine layer of particles on the pool of blood that formed from his mouth and nose, the blood green in the blue moon's lamp. Then something better than sleep, deeper, more comforting, was pulled across him, the finest blanket in the world.

HE stayed for two days, only long enough to heal his bruises, and only that long, not for comfort, but rather so he could walk long enough to get away. He had tried to go to work, only so Eva would make him stay in bed. A company doctor examined him and told him to rest and take it easy on those bruises, and Zack figured he himself could have been a doctor. The doctor asked questions about who had beaten him, and Zack knew from the rehearsed tone of the questions that the doctor asked them officially. Zack claimed ignorance.

Collie came by the second night, word having spread by then, Collie said, "all the way to Niggertown," and Zack knew how far that was exactly, having gauged by the unrest in Collie's eyes what a piece of road he had traveled to get to Zack's house, for even if this was the poor quarter of town and right next to the colored quarter, it was still the white quarter and inhospitable to Collie. Zack imagined Collie lurking along, head down, dog-beaten, showing no pride, praying to slip by. Eva left them alone to talk about it. Collie claimed he knew who had beaten Zack and claimed boastfully that comeuppance would be had, but these were a friend's lies. Although, thought Zack, there must have been a time in the history of man--one time--when a gang of black men had come across a white man all alone on a moonlit night and beat him into a pool of blood. Zack liked that thought and figured that if it were going to happen again, it might as well happen in California. Collie revealed a small bottle of whiskey, and although there was no real reason to hide it--Zack already gone-- the two friends drank as if hiding it from their mothers. When Collie left that night he said goodbye as if he would see Zack the next night; no one knew Zack was gone.

He resisted saying anything to the children except their goodnights. He knew that any expression other than the ordinary would give him away. He had reckoned, in the instant of the beating when he knew he was gone, that it would be best if his family did not know he was leaving, as if the knowing jeopardized their future. He didn't really know why he wanted them to be surprised by his leaving, perhaps just cowardice on his part, but unashamed of his cowardice, too tired for shame now. Or this: their shock at his absence might galvanize their anger against him and hold the family together, someone other than themselves to hate. He was a coward.

The next morning, after Eva had got herself and the children off, Zack left, a sack full of clothes strapped to his back, a few dollars in his pocket stolen from Eva's secret place behind the stove, a small bottle, and some tobacco. He walked south into the valley's limitless summer sun. He had stayed for the rain, the short season of lime-soaked hills and flowering fruit trees, and now the dependable drought was on. He headed towards the ocean. Collie had told him of oil fields near Los Angeles that were taking help, even old men like himself. The world always used more oil, no matter what.

He walked and hitched southward in the irrational heat, sleeping at night near the sleek, cement canals. He stole what he ate. *At least you can eat it*, he thought. In Texas and Oklahoma they had arranged it so that what was grown, cotton, couldn't be eaten by the people who grew it, saving themselves, the owners, that possible expense. Here, though, it was true, the fruit did grow on trees and you just had to reach out and grab it.

As he hiked through the valley, he grew further and further away from himself, a man who had no wife or children, no family in Oklahoma, had never farmed a day in his life. He became what lay before him, an open stretch of road, a man waiting for the next ride. Waiting in that road, he saw his life, felt its weight and boundaries, tasted it as a stone in his mouth.

If another man, another wanderer, were to have met him on that road to the southern coast and slept by the same canal with him, sharing his food and drink, and had predicted the rest of Zack's life for him, Zack would have been able to tell him accurately, at that moment, where the man had been wrong with his predictions.

If the man told Zack that he would get to the ocean and sleep on the beach for days, catching fish on an old line and cooking it there, as well as cooking crabs and clams, Zack would have agreed with him. Zack could have told the man how he would have loved the fresh, chilled salt air riding in from the ocean, this ocean cooler in the summer than any Texas gulf beach in winter. That would have been a simple prediction.

The man could have told him the following, and Zack would have agreed. That Zack would take a job in the oil fields and live in a company shack on the beach in Hermosa, breathing the beach as if it were pure ether. That Zack would live that solitary life until he went to prison because Zack knew he had one more stupid thing in him, and since he had never yet been to jail for any of his crimes, still had that coming in his life. Zack might have disagreed on the crime, thinking that the counterfeiting of silver dollars in 1947 was too stupid for anyone, but Zack would remember his ability to be swayed by the plans of others, infected by their enthusiasms, and might have conceded to the man that he might indeed be so foolhardy and wind up in a federal prison for six years. But after that the rest was easy. Returning to Hermosa after prison, grown old now in his tiny apartment, tending bar at night, listening to other people's stories and spending his days staring out of the window at the beach, until he died, alone, freed from the pain in his hands at the age of eighty.

What that fellow traveler would not have been able to predict for Zack, sitting by the smooth canal in the California heated night in 1932, was something only Zack knew. That Zack would spend the end of his life in an apartment window in Hermosa, staring at the beach, wishing he were in Modesto wishing he were in Norman wishing he were lying on the beach with Eva in Texas on their honeymoon, reliving again and again the magnificent supper they had just finished and lying with her head on his stomach, the both of them looking up at the heavens and the unending depth of stars there.

BEFORE THE SUN

DAVE TILTON

For you did it secretly, but I will do this thing before all Israel, before the sun.

2 Samuel 12:12

1

THE construction of St. Andrew's Catholic Church and School in Manteca, California, was completed in 1960, shortly after my fifth birthday. It was made of red brick, which gave rise to my childhood belief that this design would prevent the Big Bad Wolf from huffing, puffing, and blowing it down. The church became known in my neighborhood as "God's Chimney."

My family was Catholic, we lived around the corner from the church, we attended Mass every Sunday morning at nine. I began kindergarten at public school instead of St. Andrew's new school; my parents told me that I would learn more about people in a public school. My dad said this was also to compensate for not getting the kind of education received at a Catholic school. He also said that learning about how people act was more important than what is learned from books.

I was born a year before my brother Larry. He and I shared a bedroom and could see the church's bell tower from our bedroom window. We played baseball with the neighborhood kids at the diamond on the St. Andrew's School playground, after school and sun-to-sun on weekends. Once school was let out for the summer, baseball was an all-day, everyday occasion at God's Chimney.

The first pastor of God's Chimney was Father Brickman. Naturally. Father Brickman looked like Bela Lugosi's fat younger brother. He constantly smoked Lucky Strikes, my father's brand, until his luck ran out and he was diagnosed with lung cancer. Father Brickman left God's Chimney on the day that Bobby Richardson caught Willie McCovey's screaming line drive to end the 1962 World Series between the San Francisco Giants and the New York Yankees. Looking back on both events, I remember thinking they were linked, part of God's Master Plan. I had not yet learned about cause and effect.

As a result of Father Brickman's cancer, the bishop of the diocese assigned Father Selby to God's Chimney. He was slender, white-haired, grandfatherly, did not smoke, and he loved baseball. Within a week he was the umpire of our pick-up games. Father Selby taught us two important lessons about baseball. The first lesson was that a pitcher should throw the same exact pitch when a batter swings and misses, until the batter shows he can hit it. The second lesson was that a pitcher should throw a fastball *at* a batter who looked like he knew what was coming. Those of us who went to Father Selby's Masses would often discuss whether there was a connection between his baseball advice and his spiritual instruction.

The associate pastor of God's Chimney was Father Donovan. He had been the associate pastor under Father Brickman and continued his duties with Father Selby. Father Donovan was best known within the parish for his annual sermon on bearing false witness against one's neighbor.

"A man went to confession," he would begin, "and told his priest that he had been lying and gossiping about his friends. For his penance, the priest told him to get a feather pillow, go to the bridge on the outskirts of town, cut open the pillow, shake all of the feathers loose from it, and return to the confessional when he had completed this task. The man followed the priest's instructions and returned when finished. The priest then told the man to gather all of the feathers and restuff the pillow with them. The man said, 'Father, I cannot, it is impossible, the wind has blown them all away.' The priest replied, 'Just as you cannot retrieve the feathers, so it is with your false words regarding your neighbors. They, too, cannot be retrieved.'"

Every year, Father Donovan would receive a pillowcase autographed by the graduating eighth-grade class of St. Andrew's School.

Father Selby had been pastor of God's Chimney for two years when he hired The Coach to teach gym classes and coach the football, basketball, and softball teams at St. Andrew's School. After The Coach had been at the school for a few weeks, no one seemed to refer to him by his name. People just called him The Coach. He moved into his mother's house in 1964 following a one-year tour of duty in Vietnam, where he had been in the Air Force and was stationed at Bien Hoa. The military plane bringing him back to the United States left on October 29, a day before the Vietcong attacked the U.S. air base there. The attack destroyed some grounded American bombers and killed or injured numerous soldiers and civilians. The Coach returned to Manteca a few days later.

I did not meet him until he had been back in town for four years. I knew these details about him, though. Small town. People talk.

2

MR. Samuel oiled my new catcher's mitt on November 21, 1961. My dad had given it to me as a birthday gift and told me that it was always good to have a catcher's mitt handy. He gave it to me in our backyard. Mr. Samuel lived in the house behind ours. He had been looking over the fence between our backyards when I opened the box containing the mitt. He said that the leather on a mitt like mine would need to be oiled, and invited my dad and me over to oil it.

"It'll make it softer and easier to use," Mr. Samuel said to me. He scratched his head, looked like he was trying to remember something, then smiled and said to my dad, "And Samuel said to Jesse, 'Send and bring him. For we will not sit down till he comes here.'"

My dad's name was Jesse. He and I stared at Mr. Samuel.

"That," said Mr. Samuel as he began a wide, toothy grin, "is from the first book of Samuel! Chapter sixteen! Verse number eleven!" He opened the gate and my dad and I walked into his backyard.

As we headed to his garage, Mr. Samuel said, "You know, I was down on North Street today, watching helicopters put a cross up on the steeple of St. Anthony's Church. Somebody said it weighed six hundred pounds. *Six* hundred *pounds!*"

"I don't think I've even seen that church," my dad said.

"It hasn't been there long," replied Mr. Samuel. "Brand new. St. Anthony's used to be on Yosemite, was there for more than forty years until the fire. The bell from that church, as a matter of fact, is being used by the new church on North Street."

"You've been here awhile?" my dad asked him.

"Yeah," he said, "not much has changed, still mostly flat in all directions. More new houses lately, though."

Mr. Samuel opened the garage door, made a motion for us to sit on two chairs that were next to a workbench. A radio was on top of the workbench. He asked my dad if he liked Frank Sinatra. My dad smiled and nodded his head. Mr. Samuel pushed a button on the radio and we heard a man singing.

"Tony Bennett," said Mr. Samuel.

"Frank Sinatra's favorite singer." My dad smiled again.

"That's right!" Mr. Samuel replied, another toothy grin.

Mr. Samuel didn't say much once he grabbed his can of leather oil and began to rub my mitt with it. We listened to the music while he worked. After awhile he gave my mitt back to me, asked me to try it on, asked me whether it felt right. I had no idea how it was supposed to feel, but it felt right, so I told him that I liked it. He told me to keep a baseball in the pocket every night, so the mitt would get used to what was going to be hitting it. He told me to tie a shoestring around the mitt to keep the ball from falling out. My dad asked him where to buy some of that oil. Mr. Samuel told him the name of a hardware store. He turned off the radio. We went home.

My dad had a habit of writing down dates, to remember events. He wrote "11/21/61" in black ink on the thumb of my mitt. I was looking at those numbers and remembering that day while listening to the church bells at God's Chimney ringing two years and three days later. There was no school for anyone that day. President Kennedy had been shot and killed. I wondered whether the old bell at St. Anthony's was ringing. Had to be.

3

A frantic DJ announced that the Beatles' "Ticket To Ride" had entered the Billboard Top 100 Singles Chart today, which was April 24, 1965. The song was playing on my transistor radio at the moment my family and I left to see Maureen and Danny Chianti's slide show of their time spent in Afghanistan as members of the Peace Corps. Maureen was my best friend Nate Lambert's older sister. She had met Danny in medical school at the University of California in San Francisco, and they were married at God's Chimney a year later. They both joined the Peace Corps the day after graduation and were sent immediately to central Afghanistan near a town called Farah. Judging by the terrain shown in the slides, they may as well have been sent to the moon.

Nate and his family lived across the street from my family. The way Nate told the story, when they lived in Chicago his dad woke up one morning, turned on the TV set and immediately turned it off after being greeted by the theme song from "The Beverly Hillbillies," woke up the rest of the family, and told them it was time to head for California. Nate's dad got a job at the Spreckels Sugar refinery in town and worked his way up to foreman by the time Maureen and Danny returned from Afghanistan. Nate's mom called refined sugar "poison" and would use it only once a year to bake a cake for Nate's dad. She called this "the poison cake."

That year the poison cake pulled double-duty as Nate's dad's birthday cake and a "welcome home" cake for Maureen and Danny. Nate's mom later said it was the biggest cake she had ever baked. It was big enough to allow everyone who attended the slide show to have one four-inch-high piece of devil's food with chocolate frosting: Nate's parents, Maureen and Danny, Nate, Nate's brother James and younger sister Debra, Karol ("It's Karol with a 'k.'") the mother of the family that lived in the house on the corner, and my parents, my brother Larry, and me.

Larry was able to weasel a second piece of the poison cake from Nate's mom. Most of the frosting from both pieces wound up on the hip pockets of his jeans; he was notorious for wiping frosting, dip, pudding, sauce, mustard, and ketchup onto his hip pockets. This habit reached its peak when he was ring bearer in our aunt's wedding last year, and he wiped blue cheese dip onto the hip pockets of his rented black tuxedo pants before the ceremony. Very nice.

Nate's fourteen-year-old sister Debra had begun spending time after school at Karol's house. Karol was the unsolicited neighborhood voice of liberal thought. She was against the Vietnam War, for the civil rights of all Americans, in favor of most Great Society social programs, despised Nixon, and was convinced that a group of conspirators had "choreographed" – her term – the JFK assassination. She was never known to participate in any marches or activities but would interject her political views into any slightly-related conversation. So far, the only visible influence on Debra's life from her time with Karol was taking up smoking. Karol smoked Marlboros and was always eager to point out that they were originally considered a "woman's cigarette" until the "Marlboro Man" advertising campaign of the early 1960s changed that perception. Karol had kept the faith, and Debra was her recent teenaged convert.

Karol lit a Marlboro the minute Nate's dad turned out the front room lights. She shook her pack at Debra, who responded with a pair of quick head shakes without making eye contact with Karol. Danny clicked on the slide projector and began narrating the story behind each image on the screen. The screen was actually a white sheet attached to the wall with thumbtacks. I had overheard Karol use the word "subversive" in hushed tones during a recent conversation with Debra; watching a slide presentation like this one felt subversive. Like government spies.

"These rocks here," Danny was saying as an image of stacked rocks glowed on the sheet, "you'll never guess what they're used for."

"Playing army?" Larry piped up.

"No," Danny laughed, "you wouldn't want to play army with *these* rocks!"

"Danny!" Maureen giggled.

"What?" James asked.

"Well," Danny said, "this region is very poor and they don't have things we take for granted in America. Like toilet paper."

"Yuck!" Nate, Larry, James, and I chorused.

"I'm not kidding," Danny said. "Everyone in here should be lucky to be living where we do."

Karol took a drag from her Marlboro and exhaled loudly in Danny's direction.

"He's right," Maureen said, "ever since we came back, I've noticed more and more just how – "

" – many are dying in Vietnam?" Karol interrupted.

" – good we have – I didn't say it was a perfect system," Maureen continued, "and I've seen evidence of it first-hand."

"Show the next slide, Danny," Nate's dad said with a trace of irritation in his voice.

"OK, here's one of Maureen standing in front of the Taj Mahal," Danny said. "You can see swastikas on the sign next to her. They were originally religious symbols until the Nazis got a hold of them and used them for their own purposes."

"Funny how things change," Maureen said. She glanced at Danny, then back at the sheet. "Hey! What's that doing in there?" We were all looking at a slide of Maureen and Danny on their wedding day standing in front of the church.

"God's Chimney!" Nate, Larry, James, and I chorused again.

"Hey!" Nate's mom and my mom echoed.

"Oops!" Danny snickered, which gave us an excuse to laugh about God's Chimney and not have to hear about how we were being disrespectful. Our parents laughed, too, although probably for different reasons. Karol even smiled while she took another drag.

"We met one of the English-speaking locals in Farah," Danny said when the laughter had stopped, "he told us an interesting story. That's the last slide, by the way. Hope you liked them."

Nate's dad turned the lights on.

"He said that when Nixon was vice-president, he came to Afghanistan, got out of his car, took a quick look around, said there was nothing of interest here for America, got back in his car and drove away."

"Kind of hard to believe," my dad said.

"It is," Danny replied. "I checked a number of reference books on Afghanistan at the UC Berkeley library when we got back. Couldn't find mention of it anywhere. I'm sure the Federal government wouldn't exactly consider that moment a highlight of the Eisenhower Administration, if it were true. But, you know -"

" – Berkeley's not exactly a pro-Nixon kind of place," Maureen said, "and where better to find something negative about him than at the university?"

"He's gonna run for president in '68," Karol snarled. "Can you imagine that bastard as our leader? Jesus!"

"Karol," my dad said, and he reached for the pack of cigarettes in his shirt pocket.

4

NATE'S parents bought him a Sears Silvertone accordion for his tenth birthday. He had been taking lessons for three weeks when he decided to show me how he played the new Rolling Stones' song "Satisfaction" on it. We were in the garage. Nate's mom did not like to hear the accordion in the house. A few notes from it made her feelings on this matter quite clear. Nate's playing made the vacuum cleaner sound like my dad's Stan Getz records.

"Uhh-uhh, uhh-uhh-uhhhhhhhh, uhh-uhh-uhh uhh-uhh, uhh-uhh-uhhhhhhhh," Nate repeated the Keith Richards guitar theme on his accordion over and over again until I finally shouted, *"All right!"*

"Boss, huh?" he asked me.

"Boss?" I replied, "It's an accordion!"

"So?"

"*So?* Accordions can't *be* boss! They're *accordions!*"

He laughed and started playing the theme again. He tried to sing while playing, but quickly lost his place in the song and had to start again.

"Are you done?" I asked. "Aren't we supposed to play those guys The Blade knows at Sequoia today?"

"Yeah. You ready?"

"I've been ready all morning," I said, "I'm going home to get my glove. Meet you out front."

Our families lived in a new tract called Magna Terra. Every street in the tract was named after NASA astronauts: Shepherd Way, Cooper Drive,

Slayton Drive, Stafford Way, Mitchell Lane, Schirra Court, Grissom Way, Glenn Drive, and Lovell Court. We lived on Grissom Way, at the corner where the street became Cooper Drive. Nate's family lived across the street. Our houses faced each other. God's Chimney was bordered by Slayton Drive, Glenn Drive, and of course, Shepherd Way.

One of the families that lived on Cooper Drive, the Andersons, had a son named Chester. His family called him Skipper. He was the oldest boy in the neighborhood, four years older than me, and had a lot of baseball equipment that his parents had bought for him: six Louisville Slugger bats, including one with Mickey Mantle's autograph reproduced next to the bat's label; gloves; baseballs; a catcher's mask and chest protector; bases; a first baseman's glove; and a nylon bag to hold all of it. The problem with the equipment was that Skipper came along with it. He was a prick. He acted like he knew everything about baseball and thought he was the best player on the field. He did not and was not. Anyone in the neighborhood who wanted to play with his equipment had to participate during the first week of March in what he called "spring training" – pushups, situps, laps, and sprints – which he supervised with his friend The Blade, who lived near Sequoia School on the other side of town. Originally we all thought The Blade got his name from an incident involving knives; we later found out that his father got drunk one night and told him that he was as skinny as a blade of grass and twice as dumb. The name stuck.

Skipper had a paper route. He delivered the *Stockton Record* every day except Sundays. His red Schwinn Varsity bicycle had a metal rack on its back fender, which supported two blue canvas bags filled with rolled and rubberbanded copies of the *Record* for delivery. Not today, though: today was Sunday. Game day. Road trip day. Skipper had tied his equipment bag onto the rack with a rope and was waiting with the other six players to meet us. Besides Nate and me, there were The Four Johnnys – Johnny Martin, Johnny Beck, Johnny Luis, and Johnny Lewis – all of whom wanted to be called "Johnny" and would not answer to any other name; Calvin Carter, whom we called "C.C."; and Paul Newman Johnson, whose parents loved movies as much as we loved baseball.

Nate and I rode side by side, he on his black Stingray with its banana seat and butterfly handlebars, I on my red Western Auto all-purpose boys' bike. We rolled up to the Andersons' driveway. Our gloves hung from our handlebars and gently slapped against the front of our bikes' frames. I had clothespinned last year's Topps card of Mets catcher Choo Choo Coleman onto one of my rear wheel's spokes, which was supposed to make a noise resembling an engine but actually sounded like someone shuffling a deck of cards.

"Nice to see you were able to make it, ladies," Skipper sneered.

"Nice to see you, too, Skipper," Nate smirked.

"Try this again and there won't *be* a next time," he barked, "for *both* of you!"

"We better go," I said and turned my bike around. Everyone else except Skipper immediately did the same and pedaled away from the house. Behind me in single file were The Four Johnnys, C.C., Nate, Paul Newman, and Skipper at the end of the line.

We rode in that formation down Cooper Drive, turned left on Shepherd Way and passed God's Chimney, turned right on Glenn Drive, then left on Cottage Avenue and headed toward Yosemite Avenue. Halfway to Yosemite, Skipper began pedaling faster until he had passed each of us and took his place at the head of the line. Each of us gave the finger to his back.

We rode in this fashion past the almond orchards owned by Spreckels Sugar, the site of the refinery where Nate's dad worked. We could see men chopping weeds with hoes in the rows between trees. Some of the men had balanced their hoes on end against trees while they stood in the shade and ate almonds picked from the lowest branches. Nate's dad had once told me that the men who worked in those orchards would pronounce "almond" as "ammon."

Past the orchards and through the gauntlet of buildings that housed the ports of local commerce and schools on Yosemite Avenue: Hob Nob Hamburgers, Lincoln Elementary School, the Chevron gas station, Ed's Patio (rumored to be owned by the brother of the actor who played Maverick on television), Eagle's Pharmacy, Safeway, Manteca High School, Freddy's Signs, Manjo's Pizza and Chicken, Mal's Billiards, the El Rey Theater, Wrigglesworth Men's Store, The 14 Club, Turner Hardware, Mendosa's, Manteca Department Store, Central Bank, Mar's Department Store (which we always thought of as Mars Department Store), Jim's Liquors, The Scoop Newsstand, and The Lucky Lantern Bar and Grill. When we reached The Lucky Lantern, we turned right onto North Walnut Street.

Sequoia School was a block away on the corner of West Center Street and Walnut. We could see The Blade standing behind the backstop, watching the other players playing pepper and shagging flies. Skipper whistled, The Blade turned and waved to us. The other players stopped long enough to glance at us. The random soundtrack of baseball – the lazy slap of glove on pantleg, the crack of the wooden bat against the leather ball with its scores of red stitches, the chatter that means nothing and everything at the same time – all silenced for the few seconds needed for both sets of players to assess everyone on the field and the ones heading toward it. Then it all resumed without a word.

We parked our bikes against the chainlink fence that faced West Center, grabbed our gear and paired up to play catch. The Four Johnnys, as always, played four-cornered catch. C.C. and Paul Newman fielded grounders from each other, Nate and I alternated between popups and our best fastballs.

Skipper grabbed his Mantle bat and chatted with The Blade behind the backstop.

We had never played against The Blade. He had always met us at God's Chimney and usually played on whichever team had Skipper on it. Today would be different. Even Skipper was acting different. He wasn't walking around comparing himself to great Yankee managers like Casey Stengel, Ralph Houk, and Joe McCarthy. He wasn't even grousing about their new manager Johnny Keane. The Four Johnnys would refer to him as "the fifth Johnny" whenever they wanted to watch Skipper rant about how Keane was "a horrible excuse of a manager," neglecting to mention that he had managed the St. Louis Cardinals during the previous season when they defeated the Yankees in the World Series. After the Series, the Yankees fired their manager Yogi Berra and hired Keane.

Skipper waved his hand in my direction and motioned for me to join The Blade and him. I threw the ball to Nate and trotted toward the backstop. Skipper handed me the Mantle bat. The Blade and he stood a foot away from each other.

"Bottlecaps," I said, and they both nodded.

I tossed the bat toward the space between them. The Blade grabbed the thin shaft with one hand, two feet away from the knob at the end of the bat. Skipper put his hand above The Blade's, then The Blade did the same with his free hand. They repeated this until Skipper's hand covered what remained of the shaft.

"Bottlecaps," The Blade said and covered the knob with his left hand. Skipper frowned.

"We'll take last ups," The Blade said and walked toward his team. He pointed toward the infield. His teammates understood the meaning of his gesture and began to cheer as they ran to their positions on the field.

Since we had no umpire, both teams had agreed to a five-pitch limit. There would be no walks allowed, no base stealing, a foul ball on the fifth pitch was an out, and strikeouts had to be of the swing-and-miss variety. Swinging the bat was the order of the day.

C.C. batted first. He was the shortest player on our team and usually batted in a crouch, which gave him about six inches of strike zone between his chest and knees. This approach usually guaranteed a walk. Today he would have to swing the bat. He hit the first pitch up the middle and into centerfield for a base hit. We cheered wildly as Paul Newman headed toward the plate. He struck out on three pitches. None of them was even close to being a strike. Skipper, of course, batted third. He was a switch-hitter – just like Mantle – and batted lefthanded against their righthanded pitcher. On the fifth pitch he smoked a line drive right at the first baseman, who tapped the bag with his foot to double up the off-and-running C.C.

"All right, let's go!" Johnny Lewis yelled as he pulled his catcher's mask over his face. He used a Wilson A2000 fielder's glove because he did not like catcher's mitts. Johnny Luis, who pitched for us, also used an A2000.

We ran out on the field. Their half of the first inning was similar to ours: two runners on, no runs, one strikeout.

Johnny Lewis led off the top of the second by fouling off the fifth pitch. One out. I grabbed a bat and headed for the plate. I realized I was holding the Mantle bat. Skipper never allowed anyone to use that bat. I glanced at him standing where a third base coach's box should have been. He was talking to The Blade, who was playing third. I decided to use the bat and choked up two inches. It was heavier than the ones I usually used. The first pitch was right down the middle of the plate. I kept my head still, stepped toward the pitcher with my left foot, and planted my left leg at the end of my stride. I turned my hips counterclockwise toward the ball, locked my extended arms, and swung the bat with a slight upward arc, all in one synchronized motion.

The sound of the ball hitting the bat was like an explosion in my ears. The bat launched the ball like a missile into the gap between the left- and centerfielders. The ball looked like it traveled two hundred feet in the air before hitting the ground. Its splashdown was a high bounce on the outfield grass, followed by a series of smaller bounces that caused it to pick up speed. I was rounding third and heading for home by the time the centerfielder picked up the ball and threw it toward the infield.

Skipper was waiting for me at the plate, legs spread and hands on hips. He looked as mad as I had ever seen anyone who was not my dad. The Mantle bat was to the left of the plate. I bent down, grabbed the bat, and touched the plate. All of my teammates except Skipper were cheering. It was a great moment. I had never hit a ball that far.

Skipper pointed toward me. "I *never* said you could use that bat!" he screamed. His eyes seemed as big as baseballs. "Don't you *ever* – " At that moment I was finished listening to Skipper, and did not even care whether I got to play with his precious equipment again. I tossed the bat barrel-first on the ground in front of him. The bat landed and fell backward, then immediately bounced forward. The knob of the bat struck Skipper squarely in his crotch. He hit the ground like someone shot by a sniper.

As Skipper hit the ground, we all heard the loud crashing sound of metal hitting metal.

"Bad!" The Blade yelled and began to run toward Yosemite Avenue. "This'll be my third wreck this week!"

We all left Skipper moaning on the ground and followed The Blade on his one-block sprint to Yosemite. We were greeted by the sight of a white Corvair crushed on the front chrome grill of an eighteen-wheel Mack truck. The truck driver was climbing out of the cab. We stopped on the sidewalk. A crowd was beginning to gather. We could hear a siren in the distance.

"It looks like an accordion," Nate said to me.

"Yeah," I replied, "it – "

"Look!" Johnny Martin said and pointed to a head in the gutter to the left of where we were standing. I glanced at the head, jerked my body away from it, looked toward the Corvair, and saw that the driver had been decapitated. The head must have rolled across the street and stopped at the curb.

The truck driver stepped past us, took off his shirt, and covered the head. He looked at us.

"It wasn't your fault, buddy," a man yelled. "I saw it happen. He crossed over into your lane at the last second. You didn't have a chance."

The truck driver's eyes looked like they were seeing things that were somewhere else. Another man walked toward us. "You kids need to leave now," he said to us in a kind voice. "You're all gonna have bad dreams if you stay here." He put his arm around the truck driver and walked with him toward the police car that had just pulled up. We all looked at each other, slowly turned, and began to head back to Sequoia School.

"Man," Johnny Luis said to me, "you really *nailed* Skipper!"

"Fuck him," I said and glanced over my shoulder at the Corvair.

Then Nathan departed to his house.

2 Samuel 12:15

5

FATHER Selby had suggested to Nate and me that we pitch balls underhand to each other and hit them into the backstop at the St. Andrew's schoolyard as a way to improve the timing and technique of our batting strokes. He positioned Nate twenty feet from the backstop, stood at a 45-degree angle from where Nate was standing, knelt and lobbed a ball toward his strike zone. Nate swung and hit the ball in a straight line into the backstop.

"That's the way to do it," Father Selby said. "Take about twenty swings, then pitch to him. You'll probably get blisters on your hands, so be careful. Maybe get some batting gloves."

Three days later, we discovered that his prediction regarding blisters had come true. We continued without batting gloves and put Band-Aids on the popped and raw areas. We also discovered that because of our work, our swings were now level and consistent. Our teammates were impressed. Father Selby even winked at me after I hit an inside-the-park home run.

These pick-up games at St. Andrew's were fun, and so were the rituals that took place during them. They usually had nothing to do with the game itself but grew to become part of each one.

We always kept a few transistor radios behind the backstop, all tuned to the same radio station and turned up to maximum volume. Every time a Beatles song was played, an unspoken timeout was called while we scrambled frantically and grabbed bats to use as guitar substitutes, singing every word and shaking our summertime crewcut hair in the same way we had seen on TV. No game was complete without at least five Beatles' songs.

Another ritual grew from watching monster movies on TV and at the local theater. *Abbott and Costello Meet Frankenstein* was our big favorite. Someone would yelll "CHICK!" – Abbott's character in the movie – and the game would stop so we could recreate the moment when Dracula reanimates the Frankenstein monster while Costello watches, terrified and unable to yell for Chick to save him. I was always Dracula. On days when Father Selby did not umpire our games, I would use the Bela Lugosi "I vannnt to suck your blooooooooood" voice from *Dracula* and say "I am Father Brickkkkkkman!" Everyone would yell "CHICK!" and run away laughing.

Chanting at pitchers and batters, usually at the same time, was the noisiest of our rituals. No one knew the origin of "Eddie Spaghetti, your meatballs are ready" – and occasionally "Teddy" was substituted for the above-mentioned "Eddie" – but it was chanted by both teams at random. A discriminate listener could hear some of the voices saying "pusghetti" instead of "spaghetti." The defense would verbally machinegun a round of "Hey, batter batter batter batter batter batter batterbatterbatterbatterbatterbatter," while the batter's teammates would counter with "Pitcher's in a hole, ten feet deep, can't get out so he pitches with his feet." On the days without Father Selby, the words "hole" and "feet" were replaced by "rut" and "butt," respectively, until the day when one of the women who worked at the nearby parish rectory started making a few telephone calls to the parents of certain players. Mine, for example.

The most sacred of rituals, even during those prepubescent days, involved the female sex. Saying a name and linking it to a player could jumpstart anything from a homerun by the worst hitter to a wrestling match between the best of friends. Nate and I never had to worry about the former example, although the latter came into play a few times. Her name was Susan. Nate and I both liked her in that bumbling way that young boys have when attracted to young girls. Susan had a small mole on the back of her neck that was covered by her long black hair. I probably only saw the mole three or four times, random moments when I was standing or sitting behind her and she flipped her hair off of her neck for a moment. She never wore her hair in a ponytail, braids, pigtails, or a bun. The mole reminded me of a small chocolate chip, like the ones Nate's mom used during the rare times when she made cookies. I mentioned this fact to Nate; we began referring to her as Cookie during our conversations. Each promised the other to keep her identity a secret.

Except Nate did not.

One afternoon, Nate was on second and I was at bat. I saw him say something to the shortstop, who immediately called time out and motioned to his teammates to meet at the pitcher's mound. They had a brief conference and went back to their positions. Some of them were laughing. The pitcher wound up and the rest of the team began a new chant: "Eddie Spaghetti, your *cookie* is ready." The pitch landed two feet in front of the plate and the pitcher was doubled up with laughter. I sprinted past the mound, toward second base, and headed for Nate, who also was laughing. By this time everyone except Father Selby was laughing. I tackled Nate and screamed "WHY?" as I tried to punch him in the head and shoulders. Before I could land a solid punch, Father Selby separated me from Nate.

"There will be *none* of that on *this* field," he said to me, "Is that clear?"

"Yes, Father," I said and tried my hardest not to cry.

"Go home," he said, "and come back tomorrow. As for the rest of you – ," he paused and seemed to look everyone in the eyes at once, " – this will *not* be repeated. Is that understood?"

"Yes, Father," I heard mumbling as I grabbed my glove, turned, and walked away.

That night I dreamed Nate and I were teammates on the Giants. It was the bottom of the ninth in a tied game at Candlestick Park against the Chicago Cubs, he was on third with one out and I was at bat. On the first pitch I hit a rainmaker fly to the left field fence, 330 feet from home plate. The Cubs' leftfielder Billy Williams waited on the warning track for the ball to fall into his glove. Nate tagged at third and waited for Williams to catch the ball. Glove embraced ball, leather smacked leather, the crowd erupted into cheers.

Then Nate went home.

6

IT'S funny what goes through your mind when your best friend has you in a headlock. The reason for the headlock and all immediate surroundings become secondary to escape and the random thoughts that suddenly pop into focus. I had Nate's forearm around my head and found myself thinking about how Manteca stinks.

The Spreckels Sugar refinery is the main source of the odor that envelopes the town from one end to the other. It cuts through the smell of the dairy and poultry farms outside of town. It even cuts through the smell of the Spreckels cattle ranch next to the refinery. After Nate's dad comes home from his shift at the refinery, he has to remove his work clothes and change into clean ones before Nate's mom will let him in the house. His work clothes have a separate hamper to keep them away from all other clothes. No amount of laundering can remove the smell of the refinery, though, which may explain why Nate's mom refers to refined sugar as "poison."

The smell is like a mythical creature that lives in the town and keeps the townspeople in a state of undefined anxiety. I have an image of it in my mind: it's the attack of the fifty-foot-tall sugarbeet, which travels up and down Yosemite Avenue while the town's residents sleep; it peeks through cracked draperies, reads letters in mailboxes, swipes the occasional sock from clotheslines, and drapes rolls of toilet paper over mulberry trees in front yards of the town's tract homes. People die and children disappear without explanation. There is no getting away from the smell. Sort of like being in a headlock.

Nate's dad comes over to our house every now and then to watch baseball and football games with my dad and Mr. Burke, who lives down the street from us and also works at the Spreckels refinery. My dad has a portable

TV in the garage. He keeps it on a beat-up old red footstool next to a small Westinghouse refrigerator that is stocked with beer at all times. Sometimes Nate's dad and Mr. Burke come over early on weekend mornings after their late shifts at the refinery, watch some of whatever game is on TV, drink a few beers, and go home in time for lunch. My dad doesn't make them change their clothes and doesn't seem to care about how they smell or how many beers they drink. Most of the time they don't seem to care about the game as much as the beer and conversation.

On the Saturday before Nate had me in a headlock, I was cleaning the garage with my dad when Nate's dad and Mr. Burke came over. The *smell!* They both waved to my dad, he nodded and motioned toward the TV and refrigerator. Mr. Burke grabbed three beers from the fridge and turned on the TV set. The Giants-Dodgers game was on KTVU. The picture on the screen was grainy at first, but Mr. Burke repositioned the rabbit ears until it was easier to see what was happening. Lon Simmons was interviewing Giants first baseman Willie McCovey. McCovey was saying, "That's right, Lon" to begin his responses to each of Simmons' questions. Nate's dad unfolded three lawn chairs and placed them in front of the TV. My dad told me to continue cleaning the garage, took a beer from Mr. Burke, and sat down in the empty chair.

The three of them sat together for awhile, drinking beer, and watching the game. After my dad asked me to bring everyone their third beer and gave me a big gulp of his as payment for services, they began to ignore the game. Nate's dad brought up his thoughts on the actress named Anita Ekburg and her name being used in a Bob Dylan song. My dad and he began to sing that song, substituting "I need-a head, Burke" for the actress' name and howling with laughter. Mr. Burke laughed, too.

I had no idea why they were laughing, but I was aware that Nate's dad was pissing in his pants. It seemed like buckets of piss were flowing down his pant leg. He continued laughing. So did Mr. Burke. My dad stopped laughing and told me to get some towels from the linen closet and some clean blue jeans from his dresser. He had the same look on his face that I would see when I knew I was in trouble. The serious look.

I ran into the house, got the towels and jeans, hustled back to the garage, and gave them to my dad. He told me not to mention this episode to anyone. He began to wipe up the puddle near the chair where Nate's dad had been sitting. Nate's dad was unbuttoning his pants. Mr. Burke and Nate's dad had stopped laughing. My dad handed his jeans to Nate's dad, took the wet pants, wrapped them in the wet towel, and threw the bundle into the garbage can next to his workbench. He pushed down hard on the lid. I glanced at the TV and saw Giants third baseman Jim Ray Hart walking toward the plate with a bat in his hands. I wondered whether Jim Ray Hart ever sang Bob Dylan songs about Anita Ekburg to Willie McCovey and Lon Simmons. I mentioned this thought and its context a few days later to Nate, which resulted in the above-mentioned headlock.

Manteca stinks.

7

THE waning of August 1965 contained three events of note in my baseball-oriented world.

During the Giants-Dodgers game on the 22nd, Giants pitcher Juan Marichal used his bat to club Dodgers catcher Johnny Roseboro on the head, igniting a bench-clearing brawl. It happened on a Sunday, hours after Father Selby had quoted Jesus saying "...and you shall love your neighbor as yourself" during the nine o'clock Mass. We had hoped to ask him about this incident during our baseball game on Monday, but he never showed up. We played without an umpire that day.

The St. Andrew's rectory fire, according to the local newspaper, started shortly after midnight on that same Monday. It was attributed to faulty wiring. Father Donovan pulled three visiting priests from the flames and suffered second- and third-degree burns on his hands, arms, and face. He was unable to save Father Selby.

Larry and I slept through the fire. Our mom told us about it before breakfast, then asked us to say some prayers for Father Selby before we left the house to play baseball. Larry and I finished our cereal and went to the bedroom to get our gloves and bats. I was putting some toys in the closet when Larry said, "I'm glad he's dead." I hit him on the side of his head, he staggered backward until he bumped into the dresser. A statue of St. Andrew was atop the dresser; it fell to the floor, the head broke off at the neck, and rolled through the open door and down the hallway. "Now you're going to *hell*!" Larry screamed, while he rubbed where my fist had landed with one hand and wiped his tears with the other. It seemed to me that I had no choice but to perform a self-imposed emergency penance. I grabbed both pillows from our beds, cut them open with the jagged neck of the statue, and shook them until feathers filled the room.

Father Selby's memorial Mass was held on Wednesday night. The bishop of the diocese, seven priests, and two altar boys took their places near the altar. The three priests saved from the rectory fire were on the left side of the altar, three visiting priests from another diocese were on the right side. Father Donovan stood between the two groups. Both of his arms were covered with gauze bandages, and his face had red burn marks on each cheek. Each priest and the bishop hugged Father Donovan before receiving Holy Communion. All of them were weeping. Father Donovan turned to his left and put his hands on the head of one of the altar boys. Both of them were kneeling at his side.

I looked at Father Donovan's hands and thought about being with Nate in his bedroom earlier that morning. His brother James was with us. We were looking at the Topps baseball cards we had bought at Mario's Corner Store. Each pack cost a nickel, which got the buyer five cards and the worst-tasting stick of gum in the universe. Sometimes one of the cards was a checklist of other cards listed by card number and player name. That card went immediately to James, who only collected checklists. James was strange.

Nate's pack had a Giants rookies card with pitchers Dick Estelle and Masanori Murakami on it. A photo of Estelle was on the left side of the card, one of Murakami on the right. Estelle was standing in front of a scoreboard topped with red trim. The "TON" letters from the Winston cigarettes logo were visible. No "WINS." The left half of the Shell Oil logo was on the center right edge of the photo. Murakami was standing in front of a sky blue background. I asked Nate whether he wanted to trade it to me for a Tony Taylor card. It was a running joke between us: every few packs that I had purchased during the 1965 season contained a card with Tony Taylor in a Phillies uniform. I was up to a dozen of them by the All-Star break. James had seven checklists by that time.

James had been with Nate and me when we went to Mario's to buy our cards. James had pulled eight pennies out of his hip pocket and asked Mario how much his penny candy cost. Mario muttered *"Cabron!"* as he always did when James asked him questions. We always laughed when Mario used that word, although none of us knew what it meant. We left the store and saw a man walking toward the door. James walked up to him and asked, "Hey, mister – what does 'cab-a-roan' mean?" The man's mouth formed a half-dollar-sized "o" and then he sternly told us not to use that word. We laughed again. It had been a great morning for James: he had irritated two adults and gained a new checklist for his collection.

After Nate declined my Tony-Taylor-for-Giants-rookies-card trade, James left to use the bathroom. Nate shut the bedroom door and said that he had something to show me. He took his wallet out of his back pocket, opened it and pulled out a plastic baggie containing a fan-shaped leaf with seven thin jagged sections. It looked like it had been trimmed with pinking shears. He said that Debra had been growing it in the back yard, their parents found the plant, yanked it out of the ground, and put it in the garbage can. Nate clipped a leaf from the plant after his parents had finished with it. Debra had been grounded since the plant's discovery. The leaf had been in Nate's wallet for two days.

Nate put the leaf back into his wallet and returned it to his back pocket as the bedroom door opened. It was his mom.

"Seen James?" she asked.

"He's in the bathroom," Nate replied.

Nate's mom walked toward us and stopped in front of Nate. "What are you doing?" she asked him and put her hand on his head.

At the church, Father Donovan removed his hands from one altar boy's head and placed them on the other altar boy's head. Both altar boys began to weep along with the other priests. The scent of incense lingered in the air.

I was ten years old and thought I was living in a monster movie. Father Brickman looked like Dracula, Father Selby had burned to death like Frankenstein's monster, and Father Donovan was wrapped up in gauze like The Mummy. Every Mass contained a ghoulish request to eat the body and drink the blood of a man who rose from the dead. The only character missing from the pantheon of monsters was the giant mutant creature.

And then I heard a high-pitched buzzing sound. I knew no mosquito or fly could be large enough to make that noise. No one in the church seemed to be slowly letting air out of a balloon. That left only the possibility of someone trying to prevent an inappropriate sound in church by tightly squeezing both butt cheeks together. When this action failed, it resulted in what Nate called "the church fart." I also was aware that the source of this sound was sitting in the pew behind me. It was James.

I did not have to turn around to know what the rustling and shuffling sounds meant, followed by high heels clicking in counterpoint with clopping wingtips and the report of palm on face. I thought it was a safe bet that James was on the receiving end of that slap. I looked at the bishop, who was headed toward the communion rails with one of the altar boys. The people who had been seated in the front pews were already kneeling. Their attention was focused on the white host held between the bishop's right thumb and index finger, positioned over the top of his golden chalice.

8

I was playing first base. I glanced at C.C. and saw him run toward second base at the same time I heard the crack of bat on ball. Hit and run. I jerked my head toward the plate in time to see the ball hit the ground two feet directly in front of me, bounce off a hard patch of dirt and grass, then angle upward in the direction of my forehead. The ball bounced from my forehead and veered into foul territory. I felt myself fall backward and then all went dark.

I could not tell whether my eyes were opened or closed. I could not tell for sure whether I was dreaming or actually did see sugarbeets running the bases. Each beet about twelve inches tall and trailing about six inches behind the one in front of it, all chanting "Pitcher's in a hole, six feet deep, can't get out 'cause he's just a sugarbeet," then leaping into the air and exploding into thousands of tiny stars. The stars reduced their number to what looked like a dozen and orbited erratically in front of my face. I realized that I was awake and dizzy. I became aware that I was lying on my right side with my face on the infield grass. I had never given much thought to the sharpness of a blade of grass before. It felt like hundreds of sweet-smelling needles were poking my face.

"Way to keep it in front of you," C.C. said. I looked up and saw everyone on both teams gathered in a half-circle around me.

"You OK?" Nate asked me.

"Yeah," I said and stood up. "I'm fine."

"You sure?" Nate asked again.

"Yeah, let's play." I winced when I touched my forehead.

"Hey," C.C. said, "you just missed Skipper's family driving by in a U-Haul truck. You heard about his family moving?"

"Yeah," I said and punched the pocket of my glove with my right hand. "I heard his dad got transferred or something."

"He didn't even look at us," Nate said. He looked at the street and then back at me. "Maybe you should go play in the outfield."

I glanced toward centerfield and saw a huge sugarbeet positioned there. It must have been fifty feet tall. No glove. I shut my eyelids as tightly as possible. I opened them again and watched the sugarbeet spin clockwise and drill itself completely underground, leaving no trace of its having been in the outfield. I heard a tiny voice laughing "hee hee hee" at my feet. I looked down and saw one of the twelve-inch sugarbeets next to my right foot. I kicked at it.

"Ow!" Johnny Lewis said. "Whatcha do that for?"

I looked at my feet again. The sugarbeet was gone.

"Sorry," I said. "I – hey, uh, maybe we could take a break, ok?"

We left our gloves on the field and rolled the ball toward the bats that leaned against the backstop. The school building was on the first base side of the diamond. We walked toward the building and sat in the shade it provided. Some of us picked foxtails to chew the stems, some of us picked dandelions to scatter each fuzzy-looking head of seeds to the air, some of us picked blades of grass to place between our thumbs and blow like one-note saxophones, while at least one of us was on sugarbeet watch.

"Hey," Johnny Luis said to me, "I was looking at some old Life magazines at my aunt and uncle's house yesterday and there was a picture of a guy in Vietnam – some religious guy – who'd set himself on fire and was just *sitting* there."

"That's sick," I said.

"Yeah, huh?" he replied. "I mean, I don't get it, he was on fire and --"

"Monks," Paul Newman Johnson interrupted, "Buddhist monks. I used to hear my mom and dad talk about them. It was supposed to be a protest."

"Against the war?" Johnny Lewis asked Paul. "Are your folks against the war?"

"I don't know," Paul looked at his feet. "They never really talk about it much. I remember my mom asking my dad why the photographer let him burn."

"Are you kidding?" Nate asked. "That photographer knew what he was doing. It was his ticket to fame. Plus, no one else stopped the fire, did they?"

"The magazine said it was his choice to burn and he was making a point," Johnny Luis said.

"What point?" Johnny Lewis asked. "It didn't change anything, if that was his point."

"Maybe it was," Paul said to Johnny Lewis. "I don't know. What did Life magazine say?"

"I don't remember that part," Johnny Luis said.

"Buddhists do some really weird shit sometimes," Johnny Beck said and laughed nervously. "Can you imagine Jesus setting himself on fire?"

"No way," Johnny Luis said.

"But if he did," Nate said, "what better place than here at – " he paused and made a sweeping gesture with his right arm as we shouted in unison with him "– GOD'S CHIMNEY!"

"Come on," C.C. said while we continued to laugh, "let's play some more."

I got up and jogged past C.C on my way back to first base. I looked over my right shoulder and glanced in the direction of where he was still standing while the remaining players got to their feet.

"Way to keep it in front of me, huh?" I muttered.

9

THE worst part about Saturday mornings was missing all of my favorite cartoons. Bugs, Daffy, Foghorn Leghorn ("There's, I say, there's something kinda *ewwwwwwww* 'bout a boy who don't like *baseball!*" was my favorite Foghorn quote; it was my favorite quote from all cartoons), Popeye, and Bullwinkle were parts of life that I considered extremely important. I would be deprived of them on Saturday mornings in exchange for religious training in catechism class.

Catechism class was designed for Catholics in the public school system and was held each Saturday at St. Andrew's School during the school year. Usually the class was taught by a lay teacher, although one of the nuns would assist or teach the First Communion and Confirmation years of Second and Eighth grades. There would be homework, quizzes, tests, reports, and art projects on the subject of Catholicism. Report cards, including a space for grading one's conduct, were issued, signed by parents, and returned to St. Andrew's.

There were also occasional surprise visits by one of the priests. During these visits, everyone would bolt to their feet, stand at attention at the right side of their desks, and chirp "GOOD MORNING, FATHER" upon his entry and "GOOD-BYE, FATHER" when he departed.

Father Donovan paid our class a visit on the last Saturday of October, 1966. He smiled and said, "Now, let's see who's been paying attention. When Jesus performed the miracle of the loaves and fishes to feed the five thousand, how many did he have at the beginning?"

I raised my hand. "Five loaves and two fish."

"Very good." Father Donovan smiled again. "Who brought the food to Jesus?"

No one answered.

"Not sure of that one, eh?" he asked. "Well, I'll give you a clue: he had a *great* church named after him and some people – I'll bet some of them are in this room – refer to it as 'God's Chimney.' Any ideas *now?*"

"ST. ANDREW!" the class exclaimed in unison. Some of the members of the class had begun to giggle when they heard the mention of "God's Chimney," which drew a stern glare from Sister Mary Benjamin, the school principal who was substituting for our regular teacher Miss Tyson. My parents had taken a photograph of me standing with Sister Mary Benjamin on my First Communion Day. I was stepping on one of her shoes and she was kind enough not to mention it.

"Correct," said Father Donovan. "In the Gospel According to John, St. Andrew told Jesus that a boy in the crowd had five loaves and two fish, which were used to feed everyone. St. John is the only author of the four Gospels who mentions St. Andrew by name regarding this episode. Any ideas why?"

No one spoke.

"Me neither," Father Donovan smiled. "Another mystery. So," he coughed, "what else can someone tell me about St. Andrew?"

I raised my hand again.

"Are you speaking for the class today?" he asked.

"No, Father," I laughed.

"Go ahead."

"Well," I replied, "he was the brother of St. Peter and he was a fisherman."

"'Follow me and I will make you fishers of men,'" he quoted. "That was part of last Sunday's Gospel reading. It is one of the strongest images in Christianity, along with the concept of the Good Shepherd." He paused. "The Good Shepherd. This is not an image of permissiveness. The flock – *every* flock – has rules to follow or the individual sheep are abandoned and the flock itself is eventually lost. Consider a baseball team, for example. The manager runs things – he makes out the starting lineups, the batting order, decides when to bunt and change pitchers, calls for pinch hitters. Good teams are a result of good managers. Just because one team has a lot of good players doesn't mean anything if they don't play as a team. This year the Dodgers had a team of hitters with speed but not much power, outstanding pitching, and excellent defense. They went to the World Series. The Giants had so many good players like Willie Mays, Willie McCovey, Juan Marichal, and Gaylord Perry, but they couldn't beat the Dodgers, who were a better *team*. The good manager – The Good Shepherd – keeps the individuals together as a unit and playing at its bes – "

The bell rang. Everyone remained in their seats.

"Well, do I even have to *say* it?" Father Donovan laughed. "See you next week – see you *tomorrow* at Mass."

Everyone stood. "GOOD-BYE, FATHER," we chorused.

He waved and motioned for me to join him. We walked out of the room together and toward the parking lot, where parents waited to pick up their children and take them home.

"You were very good with your answers today," he said.

"Thank you, Father," I replied.

"Have you ever thought about becoming a priest?"

"No, Father. I want to play baseball."

"Well," he grinned, "you're an intelligent young man. I'm sure you'll be good at whatever you decide to do. By the way, I've been meaning to tell you – you need to work on getting in front of the ball when you're fielding."

"I do?"

"Yeah. Next time you play catch, have your buddy throw the ball on a bounce instead of a regular throw. Have him throw it to random areas – to your left, right in front of you, soft, short hop – you'll chase a lot of throws at first, but you'll get better and you can return the favor. In a game, the ball's going to go where it's going to go."

"OK, Father."

We were a few feet away from the parking lot. "Father," I asked, "if the Dodgers were such a good team, why did they lose to the Orioles in the Series?"

"Excellent pitching, Willie Davis made three errors in one inning, and it never hurts to have Frank Robinson on your team," he replied and waved to one of the parents.

10

THE Giants reacquired Mike McCormack from the Washington Senators on Halloween 1966. They needed a left-handed pitcher to join Juan Marichal and Gaylord Perry, both righthanders, so they traded relief pitcher Bob Priddy and reserve outfielder Cap Peterson to get McCormack.

Nate and I met in his driveway an hour after coming home from school on the day of the trade. We had planned to go trick or treating with James and Larry. James was going to be Batman and Larry would be Robin. Nate and I were going to rub flour on our faces, tell everyone we were pancakes, and see whether anyone would give us candy. The World Series was over and Nate was still talking about Jim Palmer's habit of eating pancakes on the days he would pitch. This ritual earned Palmer the nickname "Pancake" from sportswriters. Since Palmer was an important part of the Orioles' World Series sweep of the Dodgers, and Nate hated the Dodgers as much as any other National League team that was not the Cubs – I, being a Giants fan, was practically required by law to despise the Dodgers – he came up with this idea for a Halloween costume.

He had another idea when we met in the driveway. He was holding a baseball bat in one hand and a gunnysack in the other. He threw the bat in my direction. I yelled, "NO BOTTLECAPS!" and caught it halfway between the knob and the label. He hoisted the gunnysack over his shoulder.

"Let's go to God's Chimney," he said.

We headed for St. Andrew's baseball diamond. He told me about Paul Newman Johnson's father taking Paul to see *Cool Hand Luke* a few days before. After they returned home, Paul wanted to try and eat fifty hard-boiled eggs in one hour, just like his namesake did in the movie. His mom called it gluttony and refused at first, but they compromised and she hard-boiled a dozen eggs for him. Paul was halfway through the fifth egg when he launched its other half along with the four already in his stomach. His dad laughed and called him Cool Hand Puke. Nate and I were still laughing about it when we got to home plate.

He placed the gunnysack on the ground in front of the plate. He reached into the sack and pulled out a pumpkin with a carved jack o' lantern face: triangle eyes, triangle nose, and a smiling mouth with three rectangular teeth.

"I've been collecting these all week," Nate said, "from porches. One a day. Except yesterday I took two."

He put the pumpkin under his arm, picked up the gunnysack and walked to the pitcher's mound. He placed the sack behind the pitching rubber, took out the remaining seven pumpkins and lined them up, side by side, to the left of the mound.

"I'm Mike McCormack," he said, and with both hands he heaved the first pumpkin toward the plate. I quickly stepped into the batter's box, still holding the bat, and swung at the pumpkin. It splattered into pieces and scattered toward the infield grass.

"I'm Cap Peterson," I said. We laughed while he tossed pumpkins number two through seven toward the plate. All of them met the same fate except for number four, which was too mushy to break and slid from the bat to the plate, where it remained, looking like a deflated basketball and grinning at me with its three-toothed mouth.

"HEY!" we heard a familiar voice yell from around the corner of the school on the first base side of the diamond. It was Mr. Franklin, the school janitor. "WHAT IN THE HELL ARE YOU LITTLE BAS – "

I held onto the bat, Nate grabbed the empty gunnysack and pumpkin number eight. We ran past second base and into centerfield, heading for the outfield gate. I looked over my shoulder and saw Mr. Franklin shaking his head as he began trotting slowly toward home plate. I also saw a man standing where Mr. Franklin had been. He was staring at us as we ran toward the fence.

"Hey," Nate said as we ran, "that's The Coach."

"I'M CAP PETERSON!" I shouted as I stared back at The Coach. "I'M CAP PETERSON! I'M CAP PETERSON!"

Nate tossed the pumpkin up into the sky. We were ten feet from the gate. I glanced at the pumpkin. It seemed to hover motionless, like a popup, like a guardian angel, before it came down, and we pushed open the gate to freedom.

11

NATE and James left the public school system in 1967 and were enrolled in St. Andrew's School by their parents. Debra was already in high school by that time, but the closest Catholic high schools were in Stockton and Modesto, and her parents decided that the commute costs and time were not a good investment in her spiritual or academic life. Nate and I continued to see each other every day after school. He seemed to like his new school but was not thrilled about having to wear a uniform instead of his choice of blue jeans with shirts that were any color but white. We both agreed that the Catholic school uniform on girls was a work of genius.

Nate acquired another uniform that year when he became an altar boy. He worked his way up from the nobody-wants-to-get-up-that-early-on-Sunday 7:00 a.m. Mass to the 10:30 a.m. Mass, then the noon Mass. By Christmas he had a spot on the coveted 9:00 a.m. Mass team and got to work with The Altar Man.

The Altar Man was a junior in high school, had a full beard, some gray hair, a girlfriend named Teresa, and had been an altar boy for nearly ten years. His name was Gene Ross, but all of the altar boys called him "The Altar Man," even to his face. He did not seem to mind.

Nate and I sat in the choir loft during a noon Mass on the Sunday before his first 7:00 a.m. duty. He had found out that The Altar Man would be subbing for a sick altar boy. He said that he wanted to study whether The Altar Man did anything during a service that was different from other altar boys. When Nate was assigned a task, he went all-out to learn as much about it and do his best when the time came to perform. He also loved popcorn. We knew that the choir would not be performing during noon Mass. Mario's had recently started selling bags of popcorn, so we bought a bag and sat together in the loft. No one joined us.

"Check out The Altar Man," Nate whispered, stuffing his mouth with a handful of popcorn.

"Yeah," I whispered in reply. "Did you noticed that he shaved his beard for Midnight Mass and the Easter Vigil services?"

"Oh, sure. You *know* his mom makes him do it."

"Probably Father, too. Too bad he doesn't shape it into that Jesus-style beard with the twin beard stalactites."

"Stalagmites."

"You sure?"

"In science class our teacher said 'Stalagmites hold on with all their might and stalactites hold on tight.' So I think we're talking about beard stalagmites here."

"Maybe. Hey, how about some of that popcorn?"

"Here." Nate craned the bag in my direction. I took a handful. "Take this and eat – "

" – this is my – "

"Popcorn." Nate began to snicker.

"Hey, shut up, man."

"OK, OK."

We sat for a moment and took in the Mass. It was something that had been burned into our memories by now – fifty-two times a week multiplied by twelve years will do that to one's mind – and we were beginning to understand that there was a certain similarity between a priest saying "The Lord be with you" during a Mass and a team screaming at an opposing player during a baseball game. After a while, a person could tune out either phrase and nothing would really change. The Lord would still be with you. The ballgame would continue one pitch at a time.

"Hey," I whispered to Nate, "what do you think happens in a baseball game between two mute teams? How do you think they say 'Hey batterbatter' during a game?"

"They don't," Nate replied and motioned toward me with the bag. "They *think* it. It's even worse, knowing that everyone on the other team is thinking it while you're at the plate."

"No thanks," I pointed at the bag.

"The Lord be with you," the priest stated in a flat, even voice, followed by the deep rumbling sound of people standing in the pews below.

"And also with you." Nate and I stood and replied with the rest of the parishioners.

"What do you think of this new priest?" Nate asked me.

"I heard my folks say he's going to be the new pastor," I replied. "So what if a person grows up deaf *and* mute and never hears anyone say '*Hey batterbatter*'? Then what happens? If he can't hear the sound, does it make a noise in his head?"

"What are you *talking* about?" He took a handful of popcorn and paused. "It would *have* to."

"Why?"

"It's not baseball without it." Nate stuffed too much popcorn in his mouth and it spilled down the front of his shirt and onto the floor of the choir loft.

"Nice." I laughed into my fist.

"Yeah. It *is*, isn't it?"

"So, then," I continued, "how come you never hear major league players yelling it at a game?"

"They don't because they already know."

"Know what?"

"They know – hey, here it comes, The Altar Man's gonna ring the bells."

Like an alarm, the sound of the handheld bells near the foot of the altar rang through the church. It was immediately followed by the pounding sound of the short metal legs of the pews' kneelers hitting the floor. Nate and I watched the parishioners kneel onto the padded beige naugahyde surface. Some of them kept their backs straight, forming a right angle with their bent legs. Some of them leaned their butts onto the edge of the pew for support. Some of them did not kneel at all.

"He is totally boss with those bells," Nate smiled. "Always the same. Ding-a-ling-a-ling-a-ling-a-ling – every time."

"On the night he was betrayed," the priest said in that same flat voice, "he took the bread, gave it to his disciples, and said 'Take this, all of you, and eat it – '"

"Don't say it," I said.

"' – my body, which shall be given up for you,'" the priest continued. He took the large round host in both of his hands and raised it over his head, eyes closed, face pointed toward the ceiling. The Altar Man rang the bells again. Nate's face was a portrait of bliss. He silently mouthed the sound of the bells. I knew he was wrong about stalactites. He was also one short on the number of rings.

12

MY softball coach in eighth grade at Larkin School was Mr. Cappelletti. He was also the wood shop teacher. Every January, his standard joke was to tell the class that they would be making bats for the team. In 1968 it was no different. I had his class and heard his joke. His other standard joke was the way he would signal for a bunt during games. My teammates and I were supposed to bunt when he touched his left ear while giving signals in the third-base coaching box. There was a round growth on the lobe of his left ear. We all called it "Capp's ball" and it was the way we remembered the bunt signal. "Capp's ball means 'bunt,'" we would say to each other. "Why is he having us bunt during a slow-pitch softball game?" we would ask each other. Mr. Cappeletti liked to bunt. Some games he would have us bunt every inning.

And then Larkin School played St. Andrew's School in March and we had a new question, "Why doesn't Mr. Cappeletti change our bunt signal?" St. Andrew's knew when we were going to bunt and would be a yard in front of the batter's box by the time the ball reached the plate. Nate played on the St. Andrew's team that year.

"The Coach stole the signals," Nate said as we walked home after the game. "Every time your coach touched his ear – "

"That's it," I replied.

" – he knew you guys would bunt.'

"He's got this ball on his ear. Sometimes I think he just likes to touch it and that's why we bunt so much."

"Yeah, maybe. Kind of weird."

"He *is* weird. I have him for wood shop. Every time the bell rings at the end of class, he says 'Row one...row two...right on out.' And he says this *every* day."

"I remember hearing about this," Nate said, "and something about how the eighth graders used to laugh about how he'd tell them before each game not to drop the ball."

"He still does it!" I laughed. "But it's like he's in the desert crawling for water – you know, *'Don't...drop...the...ball...'* "

"Boss!"

"Does The Coach do stuff like that?"

"Nah," he shook his head, "he tells us dirty jokes, but that's about it. Sometimes he talks about when he was in Vietnam and Japan. Weird stuff."

"Yeah," I said, " gotta be weird having guys shooting at you."

"No, not that kind of stuff. He talks about our guys and what they did there."

"Like what?"

"I don't know," he paused, "you know, stuff like – well, whenever a girl from school walks by, he always says 'More in her than out.' He says they used to talk like that in Vietnam. Says stuff about Karen O'Brien. You know her?"

"Sort of." As far as I was concerned, Karen O'Brien was the prettiest girl in town. I'd thought this ever since I saw her singing for the first time with the choir at God's Chimney. I could not tell anyone about it, though. Especially Nate. Some lessons stick.

"He always says 'red on the head' and winks at us whenever she walks by or her name comes up."

"When her name comes up?" I asked.

"Yeah, you know," Nate replied, "just stuff. Why, you think she's boss or something?"

"Nah," I said. One more venial sin for Saturday's confession.

"Right."

"'Right on out,'" I replied in my best Mr. Cappeletti voice.

"Nice. Hey," Nate pointed toward the upcoming cross street. "Here's where The Coach lives. Want to meet him?"

"I guess. You been there before?"

"I go there after school sometimes."

We turned onto the street, walked to a sky blue house with white trim and rang the doorbell. An old woman opened the front door and said hello to Nate.

"Hi," Nate replied, "is The Coach here?"

"I'll get him," she said and shut the door.

"Jesus, is she *old*," I said.

"That's The Coach's mom," Nate said. "She's hardly ever here."

"Do you always call him 'The Coach'?"

The door opened. The Coach was dressed in the same clothes he was wearing during the softball game: white T-shirt, blue jeans, and black high-top Converse All-Stars. He came out onto the porch.

"Nice catch you made today," The Coach said to me. I was in leftfield and had made up my mind to dive for a sinking line drive. We were already more than ten runs behind at that point. If I did not make the catch, the batter had an easy inside-the-park home run. As my body extended forward and my glove opened palm-side-up to catch the ball — and I had no doubt that I would catch the ball — I felt that I could have floated in that position forever. I squeezed the glove shut when the ball hit the webbing between the thumb and index finger. Gravity pulled me down onto the outfield grass, and I heard a roar of approval from the direction of our bench and the few remaining spectators. It was the third out of the inning. Time to go bunt.

"Thanks."

"You had it all the way," The Coach continued, "that's what I was telling the guys after that play. I could tell by the way you went after the ball. No hesitation."

"Their coach always tells them not to drop the ball," Nate said. He turned and looked at me. "What did he say after you made *that* catch?"

"Nothing," I said. I was beginning to regret giving Nate that piece of information about Mr. Cappelletti.

"Yeah," The Coach continued, "you made that catch like you had an extra muscle in your legs. I grew up in the South, you know, and that's what we all used to say about the coloreds."

I had lived in Manteca for my entire life and had never heard anyone say anything about extra muscles. The Coach was at least ten or fifteen years older than Nate and me, so he must have known what he was talking about. Or maybe not.

"Extra muscle?" I asked.

"Oh, yeah," he said. I was not sure whether he was kidding.

"I've never heard that be – "

"Well, it's a fact," he interrupted and folded his arms across his chest.

"Is the camping trip still on this week, Coach?" Nate asked.

"Far as I know," he replied.

"James and I can't go. We have a family thing to do."

"That's too bad," The Coach said.

"Want to go in my place?" Nate asked me. "You and Larry? It's already paid for. It comes out of the collection plate, and your family puts in as much as anyone else. Think it would be OK, Coach?"

"OK by me," The Coach sniffed. "It's a school thing, but if you're Catholic, I don't see it being a problem with the priests."

"I'll have to ask my parents," I said. "Whether I can go, I mean. I already know I'm Catholic."

The Coach unfolded his arms. "Yeah," he said, "well, let Nate know by tomorrow."

13

HEY, *Altar Man*, I wrote, *I was really surprised to hear that you had enlisted in the Army. Everybody misses you and hopes you come back soon. How long will you have to be there? Do you know where you're going? Do you get to choose where you want to go?*

I'm in catechism class. Sister Mary Benjamin is subbing today and she thought it would be good for you to get letters from us. Beats studying for Confirmation.

9:00 Mass seems a lot different without you in it. Nate has taken over the bell-ringing duties at 9:00 Mass since you've been gone. Did he ever tell you that he and I sat in the choir loft so he could watch how you ring the bells? He does a good job. His dad bought him a camera last week. Sort of a reward.

You may have already heard that Father Zanker was named as the new pastor. Big surprise. He announced that you had enlisted during last Sunday's 9:00 Mass. People clapped. Father Donovan left for good last week. My mom and dad were talking a few nights ago and I heard them say something about too many ghosts at God's Chimney for him. He was replaced by Father Wilson. I don't know what you know about him. He seems like a good priest. During last Sunday's homily he told us about the first time he consecrated the host after Vatican II. He said that when he said the words "This is my body" and saw the faces of the parishioners, he began to understand what the church really was all about. People.

Suppose you've heard by now about The Coach getting arrested at St. Andrew's School. Handcuffed and busted by the cops during recess time. Nate was there. He saw it all and said it was like watching something in slow-motion on TV. He said The Coach didn't even act like it was a big deal. There was a story in the paper the next day – did your mom and dad send it to you? – it sounded pretty bad. Stuff about sex with boys. I never thought of him that way. Nothing like that ever happened that one time when Larry, you, and I went camping with him. Had something to do with a trip to a baseball game. That's what I heard. You know how The Coach would take some of us to games? James wanted to go and

The Coach said no. James supposedly said that he'd be sorry. The next day The Coach was arrested. There are stories about The Coach wrestling with guys my age or younger and touching them. He was supposed to have touched James. He never wrestled with me and never touched me, either. I asked Nate whether any of the stories about James were true, but he's not talking about it. You know how Nate is. He plays dumb sometimes. To me, he's not really good at it, but maybe that's just because sometimes when he's playing dumb I know why he's doing it.

Do you remember much about that camping trip? I remember we were telling ghost stories by the campfire and all of a sudden we saw these glowing eyes in the darkness looking right at us. Deer! The Coach grabbed a butter knife and tried to make a joke about it, but I think he was as spooked as the rest of us. We all went to bed that night with butter knives in our sleeping bags.

Altar Man, I thought, what do you remember about what happened when we woke up the next morning? The Coach was screaming something about how he was going to kill us. Larry was crying and begging The Coach to stop. I couldn't tell whether you were asleep or not, but you didn't make a sound. But then it got really weird – The Coach stopped screaming and began whispering, "They're here! They're here!" over and over. I remember asking him who he was talking about and it was all he could do to ask for a paper bag. I told Larry to leave and find one – no way was I going to leave him alone with a grown man acting like a nut – he came back immediately and gave it to me. I handed it to The Coach and he started breathing into it like he was suffocating. It kept him quiet and busy, though. After a few minutes he calmed down. I think he went to sleep. Larry just kept crying the whole time. I guess he thought The Coach was going to kill us all, I was thinking the same thing. The Coach had been in Vietnam – maybe he was seeing his own ghosts that morning. Fucking butter knives! Jesus! Like that would help!

Was going to ask you to be my Confirmation sponsor, I wrote, my mom and your mom thought it would be a good idea. You know how they've been getting together lately for coffee in the mornings and talking about stuff. I thought it was a good idea, too. Anyway, I guess it doesn't look like that's gonna happen now. Bummer. So, see you when you get back.

I signed the letter, folded it, put it in the envelope, sealed it, and took it up to the desk where Sister Mary Benjamin sat staring at me.

"Finished?" she asked.

14

THE detectives were twins. Their last name was Friday. Their first names were Boyd and Floyd. They were dressed in blue sports jackets, black slacks, black shoes. Boyd Friday had broken a shoelace and tied the two ends together, which is how I was able to distinguish between the two detectives.

The detectives Friday, Boyd and Floyd, were in my family's living room, telling us that they hated the "Dragnet" TV show. They were seated in two chairs that my mom had brought in from the dining room table. My dad and I were seated on the sofa. My mom stood halfway between the sofa and the hallway. I stared at Boyd's broken shoelace and hoped that no one was going to say "Floyd Friday" again. I was sure that I would laugh out loud if I heard his name. The detectives Friday began to ask me questions about The Coach. They wanted to know everything about how I met him, how long I had known him, what I did with him, how many of my friends knew him, the names of my friends, and what I knew about The Coach's relationship with James. They told my parents and me that my name had come up during an interview with what they called "one of your peers." They did not mention any names. They referred to their presence in our home as "part of an ongoing investigation."

I told the detectives that I played baseball with The Coach after school and on weekends. They were very interested in that fact and wanted to know why a grown man was playing baseball with children ten to fifteen years younger than him. I told them that I did not know why. I told them that The Coach showed me how to charge a fly in the outfield in order to get more velocity and distance in my throw following the catch. I told them that The Coach showed me that a lead from first base should equal my body length plus one step. In both situations, the idea was to gain an advantage that could mean the difference between being "safe" or "out." Floyd Friday mumbled something about being "guilty" or "not guilty," and my dad told him to knock it off. I told the detectives that I went to the movies sometimes with The Coach, The Altar Man, Nate, James, Larry, and some other guys who went to St. Andrew's School. The Coach had been taking St. Andrew's students to the movies since he had been working at the school. Boyd Friday asked me what kind of movies we went to see. I told him that we saw *2001: A Space Odyssey* last week. I did not tell him how Nate had been irritating me with his impressions of HAL saying "Dave...I'm scared, Dave..." followed by laughter and pointing at me when we were with his friends from school. I guess he was trying to be funny. Nate was really bugging me. Floyd Friday said that he saw the movie and especially liked the character of Dr. Floyd. Boyd Friday interrupted him and asked me whether The Coach ever touched anyone during these trips to the movies. I could tell that my dad was getting angry, so I quickly told the detectives that no one touched anything but popcorn. Everyone laughed at my answer.

I stared at Boyd Friday's broken shoelace and thought about coming home from Stockton after seeing *2001*. The Coach was telling us about when he had been driving his car and heard about Martin Luther King's assassination on the radio. The Coach began to sing "Bye-Bye Blackbird." He sang the first line while merging onto Highway 99, the line about talking about cares and woes, then began laughing. I imagined Boyd Friday's shoelace untying itself, which led into my remembering the psychedelic sequence at the end of *2001* mixed with the sound of The Coach's laughter repeating over and over. Something was not right. The detectives Friday stood up, thanked us for our time, gave my dad a card, and asked him to call them if we thought of something important. Just like on "Dragnet." My mom saw them to the door and said good night. My dad asked me to go to my room and finish my homework. I knew that he wanted to talk with my mom. I also knew that I would be able to hear it from my room. Larry was on a school field trip, so I had the room to myself. I shut the bedroom door, sat on my bed, and listened.

My dad asked my mom whether she had gone to the county jail today to see The Coach. She told him that The Coach had had some kind of nervous breakdown at the jail and was transferred to the county hospital. He was staying in the section with what she called "the other mental patients." I knew she was talking about nuts. The Coach was nuts! Jesus! How did *this* happen?

She said that The Coach told her about his visit from Father Zanker. Father Zanker had asked him to plead guilty for the good of the children. She repeated that phrase – "for the good of the children" – three times. Then she cried. My dad asked her what The Coach said. She said that he told Father

Zanker to fuck off and leave. I never heard my mom say "fuck" before. *Ever!* My dad asked her what Father Zanker did. She said that he left. She said something about Nate's parents and began to cry. Then neither of them said anything for a while. I put on my pajamas, turned off the light, and got into bed. I closed my eyes and imagined that I was hearing the voice of Jack Webb: "This is the city...Manteca, California...longtime locals say it got its name from a misprinted railroad ticket...the Portuguese word for 'butter' became the Spanish word for 'lard'...the mistake became the norm...when the people who live there make mistakes, that's where I come in...I carry a badge...sometimes I break my shoelaces...my name's Friday..."

The last sound I heard before falling asleep was my mom and dad walking past my door on the way to their bedroom. My mom mentioned that evening's dinner conversation and asked my dad where I would have gotten the idea of someone having an extra leg muscle.

15

I was standing behind the backstop at St. Andrew's School after catechism, waiting for Nate. We were going to hang out for a while. I had not seen much of Nate since The Coach was arrested. His family seemed to be going through a bad time. James was supposed to have been touched in his private places by The Coach. Maureen and her husband Danny Chianti had filed for divorce on New Year's Day. Debra was a senior in high school and had already been in jail three times for marijuana possession or antiwar activities. She was also spending a lot of time with Carol from down the street. Carol used to spell her first name with a "K," but legally changed the spelling a few weeks before Maureen and Danny decided to legally change their marital status. Carol told everyone that the letter "K" reminded her of the Ku Klux Klan. Nate's mom and dad were not too happy about Debra spending time with Carol instead of being at home, but they figured that it was better than her spending time in jail.

I was staring at the infield and remembering a guy named Terry who had lived across the street from God's Chimney. Terry was missing his left leg because of an operation for bone cancer. The doctors had amputated his leg. His family could not afford a replacement leg, so Terry had to use crutches to get around. He liked baseball and would show up at St. Andrew's diamond every day to play in our pickup games. He always wanted to play in the outfield without his crutches. He wanted to be like Willie Mays. We all did. Having Terry in the outfield resulted in everyone on the opposing team trying to hit the ball to wherever he was playing, so he would hop on his remaining leg and chase the ball. It was a guaranteed home run. He was a lousy outfielder, but a very good hitter. Those crutches had made his arms and wrists strong. He could hit the ball hard and always far enough so he could hop to first base. After a while, Terry stopped coming to St. Andrew's. His cancer had returned and he died. Father Zanker performed the funeral service. Nate was one of the altar boys.

I was thinking about Terry hopping after a ground ball when someone touched me on the shoulder. It was Father Wilson.

"Did I scare you?" he asked me.

"No, Father," I replied, "just thinking."

"Made you jump, though," he laughed. "You waiting for your friends so you can all play ball today?"

"No, Father. Not today."

"Not *today?*" He opened his eyes wide in mock surprise. "When I first came to this parish, I'd see you and your friends here from sunup to sundown. I said, 'Father Zanker, did those youngsters come with the deed to this property or are we going to be getting seats next to some of them in the dugout at a World Series game in a few years?'"

I laughed. Father Wilson always seemed to be in a good mood and could probably cheer up someone in an oh-for-forty slump.

"Do you like baseball, Father?" I asked him.

"Me? Nah, not much. Too slow. I like basketball."

"Really?"

"Sure," he replied, "big Celtics fan. I used to live in Boston when I first became a priest. Went to a lot of games at the Garden. Saw all the great teams with Russ, Cousy, Hondo, K.C. and Sam, Bailey Howell. Do you know what Bailey Howell used to say?"

"No, what?"

"He always would say 'It's not how, it's how *many.*' He wasn't the most graceful player out there, but he scored a lot of points. I used to get really good seats up close, too. The owners liked to see a lot of the cloth in the building," he said and winked at me.

"I like Wilt."

"Wilt's the greatest player in the game, but Russ always seems to figure out a way to stop him. What does that tell you?"

"Bill Russell is really the greatest?"

"That you should never give up," Father Wilson replied and reached into his shirt pocket. "This morning I was going through some boxes in the rectory. I found this – "

He handed me a photograph of a black man wearing an expensive suit and sitting in an airport lounge.

" – and I thought it should go to someone who would really appreciate it."

"You *found* this?" I asked.

"Yeah. Look at the back."

I turned the photograph over. Written on the back of it in blue ink was "To Father Selby, best wishes, Willie Mays, 1964."

"It's probably at San Francisco airport," Father Wilson said, "and you might want to pick your jaw up from the ground before too many bugs fly into your mouth."

"Huh? Oh," I grinned, "so where did this come from?"

"Maybe Father Selby was at the airport, took the picture, and got it autographed. Maybe somebody else got it signed for him. One more mystery. It's something we Catholics call 'our stock in trade.'"

I looked at Father Wilson. "But why are you giving it to me?"

He rubbed his forehead. "Well," he said, "I've had this in my drawer for a few days, trying to decide what to do with it. I figured that one of you ballplayers would appreciate it. You were the first one I saw. It's not how – "

" – it's how many!" I interrupted.

"And sometimes," he smiled, "it's just luck. Bye now." He waved as he turned to walk away.

"Father," I called to him.

He stopped and turned to face me.

"Thank you."

"You're very welcome."

"I miss Father Selby."

"I know you do. Some of the parents told me that he took an interest in the ballgames here. I think he fancied himself another Brother Matthias."

"Who?"

"Before your time," Father Wilson said. "Mine, too. My dad always talked about him, though. He used to tell me about a Catholic-sponsored home for wayward boys in Baltimore, where a certain Brother Matthias taught a young boy named George Herman Ruth the finer points of baseball. I guess the good brother must've done well. George grew up to be known as 'Babe.' I suppose you've heard of him?"

"Babe *Ruth?*"

"That's the one," Father Wilson replied and walked back toward the school.

I waited at the backstop for another twenty minutes. No Nate. I headed for home.

16

MY dad liked to drive on Jack Tone Road. He called it "miles of straight and a few stops." It was a two-lane road bordered on both sides by farms and ranches. The area was always very quiet. Lately I had noticed that he would always drive on Jack Tone when he had something on his mind. I had also noticed that I was beginning to accompany him on these rides. He usually would not say much to me. I think he just wanted some company.

My dad asked me to ride with him after I came home with the photograph of Willie Mays. I put the photo in the top drawer of my dresser and met him in the garage. He was already warming up the Mustang. I got into the car, he backed it out of the garage and onto the street.

It would take us about fifteen minutes to reach Jack Tone Road. I turned on the car radio and began to push the five preset buttons to find some good music for the trip. From left to right, the buttons were KSFO for Giants games and his favorite pop singers like Frank Sinatra, KFRC for Top 40 rock, KRAK for country music, KJOY for more Top 40 rock, and KSTN for soul music. KSFO and KRAK were my dad's choices. By the time I got to the KJOY button, he turned off the radio and glanced at me. "We need to talk about a few things," he said.

"OK," I replied.

He reached for his pack of Lucky Strikes, shook a cigarette loose from the others, put the end of it in his mouth, and pushed in the lighter on the dashboard. The driver's side window was rolled down. I wondered whether it would remain down or whether he intended to roll it up and fill the car with cigarette smoke like he usually did on family trips. He lit the cigarette. The window remained rolled down. A good sign.

He exhaled and sent smoke toward the windshield. "You're going to need a new suit for your Confirmation," he said, "and since you're probably going to grow out of it within the next two years, we're going to get something inexpensive but good quality. JC Penney's or Sears should have something OK."

"Yeah," I said.

"Something basic. Something Larry can wear after you outgrow it and he gets to your size. *If* he gets to your size."

We were quiet for a few miles worth of driving. He finished his cigarette, I watched some cows graze.

"Did he ever touch you?" my dad asked. He crushed his cigarette in the ashtray below the dashboard lighter.

"The Coach? No way," I said.

"Larry?"

"I – no, I don't think so. You know how weird he is about stuff," I replied and turned my head to look back at the cows.

"What about Nate and James?"

"I don't know. They've never talked about that kind of thing."

"Yeah," he said and ran his thumb across his mouth, "and why the hell would they?"

My dad was cussing. Not a good sign. "What's going to happen to The Coach?" I asked.

"He's done working with kids, for starters," He took another cigarette from the pack, put it on his bottom lip but did not light it. The cigarette bobbed up and down with each word and stayed in place from a combination of spit and practice. "I don't know, really. Your mother had been going to see him but isn't going anymore."

"Why?"

"Because she doesn't know whether he did it or not."

"Do you think he did?"

"Here's what I think," he pushed the lighter in. "I think he had you kids convinced that he was the fucking pied piper and whatever he said was pure *gold*. One of you didn't get his way and decided to shit all over the whole program. Whether he's a goddamned pervert or not doesn't *matter* now. His life's ruined."

He lit his cigarette and exhaled.

"And James and Nate," he continued, "that whole family – Jesus *Christ!* – they need to get those kids to some kind of counseling program and *fast*. He gives me the creeps."

"James?"

"You think he's normal?"

"He's just a kid," I said and stared at him.

"Not any more."

He made a left turn at the next cross street and headed for home. We said nothing for the rest of the trip until he pulled the car into the driveway.

"Things are going to be different between you and Nate," he said. "Everything has changed. I'm sorry for both of you. You seem to be good friends."

"We are," I said.

"That family is going through a lot of trouble right now. Be his friend but don't push it."

"Thanks, Dad."

He coughed. "If you know something, I need to know."

"I don't."

"OK." He opened his door and got out of the car.

I stared at the garage wall and thought about the camping trip. It was morning somewhere in the Sierra Nevadas. The Coach had found the area on a U.S. Army survival training map. There were no other campers in sight. The Altar Man was either asleep or faking it. Larry was bawling his eyes out. The Coach had a paper bag over his face and was breathing in and out, over and over. I kept whispering to Larry that everything was going to be all right and wondered if The Coach was going to breathe into that bag until it killed him. I tried not to think about whether The Coach was going to kill us. He dropped the bag. I watched it fall from his face and land on the canvas floor of the tent. The Coach was asleep. I motioned to Larry to quietly get out of the tent. He did. I tapped on The Altar Man's leg until his eyes opened. I put a finger to my mouth and motioned toward the tent flap. The Altar Man got up and followed Larry. I picked up the bag and left the tent. I went behind the redwood tree near our campsite and threw up in the bag. I rolled up the bag, walked to The Coach's car, got the keys out of the ignition, and opened the lid to the trunk. I put the bag into the back of the trunk and gently closed the trunk lid. Larry had stopped crying. I looked at The Altar Man and knew that he had been faking sleep in the tent. I heard three quick taps on the Mustang's trunk, glanced at the rearview mirror, and saw my dad making the umpire's "out" sign. I reached for the door handle.

17

LARRY and I were in the front room watching "Davey and Goliath" on TV. It was an episode titled "The Polka-Dot Tie." In it Davey and his claymation friends reject a claymate named Nat because they don't like his tie. The episode's big lesson was all about how God accepts everyone.

"Oh, Dayyyyyyyyyy-veeeeeeeeeeee!" Goliath said in a voice that only Davey and the TV audience could hear.

"Oh, Dayyyyyyyyyy-veeeeeeeeeeee!" Larry and I mimicked and laughed. We always did.

"How come Gumby and Pokey never go and play with Davey and Goliath?" Larry asked me.

The front doorbell rang. My mom walked from the kitchen to the front door.

"Probably because they don't go to the same church," I replied as the front door opened.

"Hi, Nate," my mom said, "come on in. They're watching cartoons."

Nate wiped his feet and entered the room. He wore blue jeans, a white T-shirt, and black Converse high-top sneakers. He looked like a younger version of The Coach.

"Hey," Larry said.

"Hey," Nate nodded in our direction. "Sorry I haven't been over lately. Been kind of, you know, stuff going on." He sat down on the floor next to Larry, who was a foot away from the TV.

"Yeah," I said.

"What's Davey done this time?" Nate pointed at the TV.

"You know, the usual thing," I replied, "then he gets the big lecture about God from his dad and everything's fine at the end."

"*Oh, Dayyyyyyyyy-veeeeeeeeeeee!*" Larry moaned.

"Why don't you leave?" I said to Larry. It was more of a command than a question.

"Mom!" Larry yelled.

"Larry!" she yelled back.

"Yeah," Nate said, "the big lecture. Lots of them around the house lately."

"Yeah?" I asked.

"Yeah. All of this God stuff."

"Nate?" my mom asked as she reentered the front room. "Would you like something to eat?"

"No, thanks," he replied.

"Larry, I need you to come with me," she said. She looked at me, then back at Larry.

"Mom," Larry began but was interrupted by a sharp "Now!" from my mom. He got up slowly from his spot on the floor and dragged his feet all the way into the kitchen. Nate and I could hear her telling him not to sit so close to the TV.

"Are you still getting confirmed?" Nate asked me.

"Yeah, sure," I said. "You?"

"I don't know. I guess."

"Yeah. Hey," I pointed at him. "New clothes?"

"Yeah."

We said nothing for the next few minutes. Nate turned around and watched the TV. I watched him. "Davey and Goliath" ended and a commercial for Cheerios followed it. Nate turned and faced me.

"The folks are really going on and on about God this and God that," he said, "I think it's for their own benefit so they don't feel like failures, because…"

"James?" I interrupted.

He was silent again. He looked calm, as though he had already made up his mind about something.

"You ever wonder about all of this stuff in the Bible that we hear about every week?"

"Like what?" I asked.

"I mean, like that part where John The Baptist baptized Jesus and everyone there heard a voice saying 'This is My Beloved Son.'"

"So?"

"So what if it was bullshit? Or what if it really *was* God and He was talking about someone else?"

"Like who?"

"I don't know. It doesn't matter."

"Well, *sure* it does. It's about God."

"*Oh, Dayyyyyyyyyyy-veeeeeeeeeeee!*" Nate mocked. "Look at the whole thing. Jesus taught something that was different from what was accepted as the truth. He gets arrested and executed. Nothing really changed. What's the big lesson? Not 'Love God and your neighbor as yourself.' No. The big lesson is 'Do what we tell you or we'll find a way to get rid of you.' Look at – "

"The Coach?" I interrupted again. "Where'd you get all this? From him?"

"Fuck you."

"Fuck *me*?" My voice was beginning to rise in pitch.

"You don't even know."

"I don't even *care*! Just get out of here, all right?"

My mom came in from the kitchen. "Everything OK in here?"

"Yeah, sure," I said. Nate stared at the TV.

"Will you take the garbage out for me?" she asked.

"OK."

I got up and walked toward the kitchen. I did not even look at Nate. I grabbed the bag from under the sink, walked out of the house and into the back yard, lifted the garbage can lid, threw the bag into the can, mumbled "Fuck *you*, Nate," put the lid back on the can, and returned to the house.

My mom was standing at the sink, rinsing a glass. "Nate left," she said. "He asked to use the bathroom, went down the hall, and left within seconds. Did you two have an argument?"

"No," I lied. I did not feel like hearing a lecture on the subject of friendship, so I added one more venial sin to my growing list for next Saturday afternoon's trip to the confessional at God's Chimney. It would join the usual entries of "disobeyed my parents," "had impure thoughts about Karen

O'Brien," "used the Lord's name in vain," and the ever-popular "made my brother angry."

"I didn't hear the toilet flush, though," my mom said. "Would you mind checking it?"

"Sure," I said. I walked toward the bathroom and hoped that Nate had not left a lovely parting gift for me in the bowl. I lifted the lid and saw nothing but water. I glanced at the bedroom I shared with Larry. The top drawer of my dresser had been pulled open. I always kept it shut. Larry had never shown any interest in its contents. Maybe things had changed.

I walked into the bedroom, looked into the opened drawer, and saw that the Mays photograph was gone. In its place was Nate's baggie containing the crumbling marijuana leaf from his sister's plant. Nate must have been planning to take something of mine, opened the top drawer, and hit the jackpot. He did not know where I kept the photograph. No one did. Sometimes you get lucky, just as Father Wilson said to me on the day he gave me the photograph.

I put the baggie in my pocket, closed the drawer, went across the street to Nate's house, and knocked on the front door. Debra answered it. She told me that no one was home, and she had not seen Nate since breakfast. Lucky me.

18

ALL I remember was church bells ringing all day long and we stayed home from school. Why?" I whispered. The lights were out, Larry and I were in our beds. It was a school night. "It's for my homework," Larry whispered back. "What did we do?"

"Our family?"

"Yeah."

"I don't know. It was five years ago. Mom cried. Dad stayed at work. Like he does now. You and I played with our toys. Mom kept opening the door and asking us to be quiet. You know, because he was the President."

"Do you think his brothers are going to be killed?"

"I hope not."

"Me neither – do you think Nate's dead?"

"I don't know."

"He's been missing for ten days."

"Yeah."

"Where would he go?"

"Maybe he's hiding."

"Why?"

"Keep your voice down," I hissed. "I don't know. It probably has something to do with The Coach and James. You know, whether it happened or not."

"What did the cops ask you about him?"

"Just stuff. They think I was one of the last from the neighborhood to see him before he, you know, took off. Didn't they talk to you?"

"No. Maybe he's with The Altar Man."

"The Altar Man's on his way to Vietnam. Probably there by now."

"Oh, yeah."

"You know what? I don't think The Coach did what everybody thinks he did."

"Do you think James is lying?"

"I think whatever he told his parents and the cops has been turned into something else and James can't get out of it."

"Why?"

"Maybe he likes the attention. Maybe it has to do with his parents. Maybe the school didn't like The Coach and needed a reason to get rid of him."

"But Nate says he's a good coach."

"Yeah. That's what he says."

"Go to sleep!" my mom yelled from the front room.

19

MY folks took Larry and me to lunch at Molly's Restaurant two weeks before my Confirmation. The hostess seated us at a table near the counter. One of the waitresses behind the counter was talking to an old man who was sitting next to three young men. The three men looked like they were teenagers, or maybe in their early twenties. The waitress called the old man "Tahoe."

"So, Tahoe," she said, "how's your wife these days?"

"Well," he said, "I came home last night. She says to me, 'Drunk again.' I say, 'You too?' Uh-*hee*-hee-*hee*-hee-hee!"

"Been to Tahoe lately?" one of the three young men asked him.

"Oh, yeah," Tahoe replied, "I'm always on the road. I've been in nineteen states."

"Yeah?" the young man smirked. "I've been in thirty-one states."

"Well, uh...uh..." Tahoe stammered, "I've been in *all* of them – and *Alaska*!" The three men burst into uproarious laughter at Tahoe's response. Tahoe smiled, sipped his coffee, and did his "uh-*hee*-hee-*hee*-hee-hee!" laugh. It sounded more like hiccups than laughter.

"Three wise asses," my dad muttered, "they'll be laughing it up real soon, once Uncle Sam dumps their sorry butts in the jungle."

Larry could not prevent himself from snickering when he heard an adult say the word "butt." Today was no exception.

"You think it's *funny*?" My dad glared at Larry, who immediately stopped laughing, shook his head, and looked at the tabletop.

"Who's having what?" my dad asked.

"A cheeseburger and fries and a Coke,' I said.

"I think that's what I'm having, too." My mom smiled at my dad and touched Larry on the shoulder. She looked at my dad, then back at Larry.

"Larry," my dad said in a soft voice.

Larry looked up from staring at the table. Before my dad could continue with whatever he wanted to say, the waitress came to our table and asked whether we were ready to order. We were. We did.

The waitress walked toward another group of tables. My mom absentmindedly traced the length of her right cheekbone with her right index finger and said, "I talked with Teresa Josephson's mother today. She told me that Gene Ross went AWOL. Can you believe that?"

"Jesus," my dad muttered and shook his head.

"She said that the military police don't seem to know where he is," my mom continued, "I hope he's not hurt."

"He'd better hope the MPs don't hurt him," my dad said. He glanced at his coffee cup.

"Weren't you thinking about him as your sponsor?" she asked me. I nodded. "Well," she said, "I think your Uncle Jimmy will be a good sponsor. I think he got a kick out of both of you having the same Confirmation name."

"What does it mean that The Altar Man's a wall?" Larry asked.

"Not a wall," my dad said, "AWOL. Absent Without Official Leave."

"Oh," Larry replied and paused. "But I still don't get it."

"He left without permission," I said and stood up.

"Ohhhhhhhhhh," Larry said.

"Where are you going?" my dad asked me.

"Bathroom," I said and headed toward the restroom area marked "GENTS" in black capital letters over the door.

I pushed the door and entered the restroom. A man was using the urinal. I recognized him immediately. It was Danny Chianti.

"Hey, Danny," I said.

He glanced over his shoulder. "Hey! How's it going?"

"Good," I smiled. "Haven't seen you around for awhile."

"Yeah, I was visiting my in-laws – my *former* in-laws, I should say."

"Yeah. Sorry to hear about that."

"Yeah. Funny how things change." He zipped up his fly and flushed the urinal. "Anyway, I thought they might need some help or support, considering the recent developments in the family. Know anything about Nate?"

I shrugged my shoulders.

"I always wondered why you two were friends," Danny said. "I don't mean that in a *bad* way – I just thought you both had different interests. Except for baseball."

"I never really thought about it,' I replied, "I – his family moved across the street and my mom suggested that I go make friends."

"Well, you were good friends," Danny said, "I hope you can be friends when he returns."

"He took something of mine, Danny."

"Really?"

"Yeah. It was more of a trade without *asking* me."

"Hmmmmm," he grunted.

A flush came from the toilet stall. We listened to the sounds of someone pulling up his pants and buttoning them, zipping his fly, and unlocking the stall door. The door opened. A man with Middle Eastern features came out of the stall. He was wearing a blue windbreaker and holding a notebook. He walked by us and dropped his notebook. It landed pages-up on the floor.

"Hey," Danny said to the man, "you dropped your notebook."

The man stopped and turned around. Danny walked to the sink and began washing his hands. The man bent down, picked up the notebook and closed it. His windbreaker was unzipped low enough for me to see that he was wearing a shoulder holster with a small pistol in it. He nodded his head sharply in my direction, turned, and quickly exited the restroom.

"Nice guy," Danny said. He turned off the water and dried his hands on a paper towel.

"Uh-huh," I replied.

"Well, you know the old saying, 'No good deed goes unpunished.'" He grinned. "Wonder which of the three of us is going to get punished?"

"Maybe it'll be someone else."

"Maybe. I was never all that clear on how that old saying worked. Are you here with your family?"

"Yeah."

"Then you'd better get back with them or *you're* gonna be the one who gets punished."

"I guess so," I laughed.

Do me a favor," he said, "and don't mention that you saw me. I'm gonna leave through the bar, so they won't know I'm here."

"OK," I said, "but is something wrong?"

"Not a thing."

We shook hands. I left him in the restroom and returned to the table where my family was seated. My dad was smoking a cigarette and drinking coffee. Larry was reading the label of the ketchup bottle. My mom was looking in the direction of the parking lot. I sat down in my chair. My mom asked me whether I had seen a nervous-looking man with dark skin in the restroom. The waitress was headed toward our table with an armful of plates. Tahoe coughed.

20

LARRY was sitting on his bed, picking his nose. I was on my bed, looking through my scrapbook of the Giants' 1965 baseball season. I was reading a newspaper article with the headline "SF GIANTS ENJOY FIRST VISIT TO HOUSTON'S ASTRODOME BY WINNING, 8-1." It was dated May 22. I had cut it out of the *Stockton Record.* The article was about Ron Herbel's second consecutive winning start in ten days and his first major-league hit. I had listened to that game on KSFO. It was not as memorable as the game two years later, when he hit a double, tried to stretch it into a triple, and was tagged by the patiently waiting third baseman for the third out of the inning. The Giants radio announcers, Russ Hodges and Lon Simmons, laughed hysterically during the entire play, from hit to out.

The article went on to describe Herbel losing his shutout on a homerun by Astros catcher Johnny Bateman late in the game. The Astrodome scoreboard proceeded to run a series of animated segments, featuring fireworks, a "GO TEAM!" logo, and the Texas flag. "Herbel and his catcher, Tom Haller," the article stated, "stood transfixed on the mound and refused to continue until they had seen the entire show."

I looked up from my scrapbook to see Larry wiping his finger on the wall behind his bed.

"Are you saving them for a reason or just waiting for Mom to find them?" I asked him. He smiled and began working on the other nostril.

I returned to the last paragraph of the newspaper article. "Haller made a little history of his own in the ninth," it stated, "when he batted right handed for the first time in his career. He struck out." Tom Haller's brother Bill was an umpire in the American League. I wondered whether either of them ever did any pick-and-wipe when they were younger. Or now.

Transfixed on the mound. I shut my scrapbook and remembered a dream I had last night. I was climbing onto the roof of my family's house to retrieve a baseball. The ball was floating in a tub of gold. Suddenly the ball was gone and in its place was Karen O'Brien. Standing. Totally naked. The Coach was right about "red on the head."

"Larry," I said, "do you remember the first Giants game Dad took us to?"

Larry's finger froze in his nose as he waited for me to continue.

"It was 1964 or 1965. They played the Cubs."

"We took Nate with us," Larry said.

"Uh-huh," I replied, "and Cap Peterson got a single in the fifth or sixth to break up a no-hitter."

"He did?"

"Yeah. Our first Giants game. Mays and McCovey didn't homer once and *Cap Peterson* gets their first hit!"

"So?"

"*So?* That's like The Beatles letting Ringo sing every song! And then Nate convinced you to be a Cubs fan!"

"I like the Cubs," Larry smiled.

"The Cubs will never win. *Nev*-er," I said.

"Oh, like *you* know," Larry said.

"I know you might wanna pull your finger out of your nose," I said and tossed my scrapbook onto my pillows.

Larry mimicked someone totally lost in thought, gave his picking finger a quarter-turn while making a creaking door sound, then removed it from his nostril. He stared at the finger with a disappointed expression on his face. I was not sure whether the expression was genuine or not.

"Larry," I paused, "you didn't take my Mays photo, did you?"

"What Mays photo?"

"The one in my dresser."

"No."

"Don't tell anybody," I said, "but I think Nate took it."

"When?"

"The day he was over when we were watching 'Davey and Goliath,' remember?"

"Yeah."

"Somebody opened my top drawer, took the photo that was there, and replaced it with a pot leaf."

"Nate smokes *pot?*"

"I don't know," I said, "but I know he has a leaf. Or had one."

"Boss!" Larry exclaimed. "Do you have it now?"

"I got rid of it. And when did you start saying boss?"

"I don't know," he said, "so what if I am?"

"No one says that anymore."

"I do."

"Since when?"

"What do *you* care?"

"Forget it," I said, "it's not that big of a deal."

"Cap Peterson," Larry said and began to laugh. I ignored him and resumed thinking about Karen O'Brien in the tub on the roof. I wondered whether a dream image would be disappointed in me for lying about the pot leaf that was in my wallet.

21

I went to the St. Andrew's School baseball diamond after lunch on the day of my Confirmation. It was the last Saturday of May 1968. No one was there. Catechism classes were finished for the year. Pick-up baseball games at this diamond had become rare occurrences, since most of us were playing on Little League or Babe Ruth League teams. We were beginning to move in separate directions.

Home plate was gone. In its place between the two batters' boxes was a group of thirty white communion wafers arranged side-by-side in the standard pentagon shape of the plate. There were three rows of seven, a row of five, a row of three, and one wafer that pointed toward the backstop. The sky was filled with dark nimbus clouds, which was unusual for this time of year in the valley.

I stared at the wafers and wondered who put them there, why they were there, and whether they had been consecrated. I could see a cross and "IHS" logo stamped onto the center of each wafer. I heard a rumbling sound coming from beneath the wafers. I sprinted toward first base, looked over my shoulder, and watched as a giant sugarbeet, spinning counterclockwise and making a "hee hee hee" sound, rocketed into the sky, and vanished immediately. I ran back to where I had been and knelt in front of the home plate area. The ground appeared to be untouched. As my knee hit the ground, rain began falling. Hard. I watched the wafers melt into long gooey strands, spin like clothes in a dryer, and remold into the five-sided plate.

As the rain fell and my clothes became increasingly soaked with each passing second, my thoughts returned to the Confirmation Mass. The first reading of the Mass was from the twelfth chapter of the Second Book of Samuel. Nate's dad, Mr. Lambert, read it.

Then the Lord sent Nathan to David, Nate's dad began, *and he came to him, and said to him: "There were two men in one city, one rich and the other poor.*

"The rich man *had exceedingly many flocks and herds.*

"But the poor man *had nothing, except one little ewe lamb which he had bought and nourished; and it grew up together with him and with his children. It ate of his food and drank from his own cup and lay in his bosom; and it was like a daughter to him.*

"And a traveler came to the rich man, who refused to take from his own flock and from his own herd to prepare one for the wayfaring man who had come to him; but he took the poor man's lamb and prepared it for the man who had come to him."

Then David's anger was greatly aroused against the man, and he said to Nathan, "As the Lord lives, the man who has done this shall surely die!

"And he shall restore fourfold for the lamb, because he did this thing and because he had no pity."

Then Nathan said to David, "You are the man! Thus said the Lord God of Israel: 'I anointed you king over Israel, and I delivered you from the hand of Saul.

'I gave you your master's house and your master's wives into your keeping, and gave you the house of Israel and Judah. And if that had been too little, I also would have given you much more!

'Why have you despised the commandment of the Lord, to do evil in his sight? You have killed Uriah the Hittite with the sword; you have taken his wife to be your wife, and have killed him with the sword of the people of Ammon.

'Now therefore, the sword shall never depart from your house, because you have despised Me, and have taken the wife of Uriah the Hittite to be your wife.'

"Thus saith the Lord: 'Behold, I will raise up adversity against you from your own house; and I will take your wives before your eyes and give them to your neighbor, and he shall lie with your wives in the sight of this sun. For you did it secretly, but I will do this thing before all Israel, before the sun.'"

Then David said to Nathan, "I have sinned against the Lord." And Nathan said to David, "The Lord also has put away your sin, you shall not die.

"However, because by this deed you have given great occasion to the enemies of the Lord to blaspheme, the child also who is born to you shall surely die."

Then Nathan departed to his house.

"This is the Word of the Lord," Nate's dad said at the end of the reading. A tear ran down his right cheek. I noticed some other parishioners were also weeping.

Everything that followed the reading was a blur until I knelt before the bishop. I remember Father Zanker stood next to the bishop. I remember the bishop anointed my forehead, touched my cheek, and blessed me. I remember I stood up and discovered that the bishop had one of his feet on my red robe, which proceeded to rip down the middle as I assumed a standing position. The bishop looked directly at me and said, "Repent."

And now, drenched in not-quite-summer rain, I wanted to reflect upon my confirmation and new status as what the Church called a "soldier of Christ." Instead, I reflected upon the fact that I suddenly felt let down by Catholicism and did not understand why. I felt as AWOL from the army of Christ as The Altar Man was from the U.S. Army. I thought that having my robe ripped was a sign. It felt like I had been torn and removed from what I had known about God since childhood. Maybe Nate was right about nothing changing. Maybe it was the end of a cycle that began when I stood on Sister Mary Benjamin's foot on the day of my First Communion. Maybe something had clicked in my mind to make me realize that the whole idea of God was a shared lie designed to bypass the loneliness of days filled with a meaningless existence and followed by an eternal blank space. No heaven, no resurrection, no being seated at the right hand of the Father. No way to know the answer until it was time to die. Faith was not an answer. Faith was a diversion. Faith got lambs killed. The only thing about God that still made sense was as the beginning of all things. Something powerful enough to create the universe did not need an army. Or anything. Or anyone.

22

THE Coach was sitting on the porch at his mom's house. I saw him there as I was walking home from Mario's Corner Store. He had something in his hands that looked like a square foot of wood or cardboard with a picture on it. He was staring at the cloudless blue sky.

I walked toward the house. A rubberbanded copy of the *Stockton Record* was still on the lawn. I picked it up and walked up the three stairs to the porch. He did not look at me until I stood directly in front of him.

"Hey, Coach," I said, "how's it going?"

"Feel like gettin' some," he said. His mouth twitched from a quick grin to a blank stare. "You?"

"OK, I guess," I said. "I heard you were in a hospital."

"Yeah. Your mom came to see me a few times."

"Yeah."

"Then she stopped."

I looked at the square object in his hands. It was a copy of The Beatles' *Yesterday and Today* album.

"Been listening to that?" I asked. His mouth made that quick twitchy grin again. I wondered whether it was a result of his stay in a mental hospital or was caused by some kind of medicine that he had to take as part of his release from the hospital.

"I got this in Japan after I was finished with my tour in country," he replied. "Seen this before?"

"I have it."

"Not this one." He peeled the cover downward from the upper right hand corner to reveal a different picture. The Beatles were wearing white lab coats with red stains. They were holding dolls stained with the same red color, and chunks of red meat. They were not dressed to appear on "The Ed Sullivan Show."

"The record company decided they didn't like this cover after it had been manufactured and shipped to stores," The Coach said, "so they pasted a new cover over the ones that hadn't been shipped yet."

"Wow!" I exclaimed.

"Things aren't always – " he began, then he stopped and resumed looking at the sky.

"I guess," I said.

We were silent. Finally he lowered his eyes and looked at me again.

"What do you want?" he asked.

"I – "

"Did you come here to find out whether I *did* it?" he hissed.

"I saw you sitting on the porch," I said, annoyed. "I came over to say hi."

The Coach looked at his feet. He was wearing what looked like the same black high-top Converse All-Stars he was wearing when I met him, along with his familiar uniform of white T-shirt and blue jeans. He always wore the same clothes.

"All of the charges were dropped," he said. He rubbed the top of his head, shook it once, and looked at me. "Except for one. Contributing to the delinquency of a minor."

"For what?"

"Anything I said to a kid that had to do with sex."

"Anything you *said*?"

"Yeah. You know, like that story I told you once about those two guys in a Da Nang Quonset hut who dragged each other by their – "

"Uh-huh," I interrupted. It was way more than once, I thought.

"Like that. Anyway." He paused and rubbed the top of his head again. "Seen Nate?"

"He's gone," I replied. "No one knows where he is."

"What a dick he turned out to be," The Coach said. "Jesus!"

"Do you know where he is, Coach?"

The front door opened and The Coach's mom stood in the doorway. She motioned for him to come inside. He rose to his feet, still holding his Beatles album, and turned to face his mom and the open door.

"I don't know," The Coach said without turning to face me. He walked past his mom and into the house.

The Coach's mom remained in the doorway. I handed the newspaper to her. "Thank you for coming by," she said. "He always speaks well of Nate and you." She shut the door slowly. I stared at the door for a few seconds, then turned and headed for home.

I passed by God's Chimney and saw a side door propped open. I could hear a soprano voice singing inside the church. I headed for the open door. There was a soundproofed chapel with clear glass windows in that part of the entryway. It was known as The Crying Room. Parents would take their bawling infants and small children there so the other parishioners would not be distracted or bothered by the noise during Mass. Speakers were mounted on the wall to broadcast the sounds of the Mass into the chapel. A clock was on the wall above the windows. I walked into The Crying Room and looked through the windows for the singer.

It was Karen O'Brien. She was kneeling in front of the cross behind the altar. I recognized the melody as the hymn "Humbly We Adore Thee." Karen was singing it in Latin. I sat in a pew and closed my eyes. Her voice sounded as beautiful as ever. The last thing I remember before drifting off to sleep was her singing "Jesu, quem velatum nunc aspicio, oro fiat illud quod tam sitio" and my hope of returning to that dream of her in the tub of gold on the roof of my parents' house.

When I awoke, she was gone. The inside of God's Chimney and The Crying Room were dark. I could barely see 12:35 on the clock. I got up from the pew, exited the church, and ran home.

I opened the front door and saw my mom and dad sitting on the couch. She turned her head and looked at me. Her face was swollen from crying. My dad had his arms around her. The TV was on. I figured that I was in deep trouble for coming home so late. She buried her face in his shoulder. He looked up at me.

"Senator Kennedy was shot in Los Angeles," my dad said.

23

MY mom had taken Larry out to shop for new clothes, my dad was at work, and I was the only one home when the mail arrived. It had been a week since Robert Kennedy died. No one else saw the letter addressed to me in an envelope from the Ambassador Hotel in Los Angeles. Underneath the preprinted return address was "THE PROPHET NATHAN" written in blue-inked capital letters. I recognized the handwriting immediately.

I opened the envelope and found a photograph wrapped in Ambassador Hotel stationary. The stationary bore the words "We did it! We did it!" They were written in the same ink and handwriting as on the envelope. The photograph was of a man and a woman. In the background were a potted plant and expensive-looking furniture. I assumed it was taken in the hotel lobby. The woman was wearing a polka-dot dress. Her arms were in a swinging position, as though she had been running. Her face was not in the picture. None of her head from the neck up was in the picture. The man next to her also appeared to have been running when the photograph was taken. His face was in the picture. I recognized his clean-shaven face. It was Gene Ross. The Altar Man.

The handwriting on the stationary and envelope was Nate's.

I was not sure why I had received this letter. I knew that Robert Kennedy had been shot at the Ambassador Hotel. I recognized the newspaper photos of his assassin as the Middle Eastern man in the Molly's Restaurant restroom with Danny Chianti and me. I had listened to Carol talk about the theories concerning a woman in a polka-dot dress with a man leaving the Ambassador Hotel yelling "We did it! We did it!" after Kennedy had been shot. But what was The Altar Man's connection to the event? Was he part of a conspiracy? Was Danny Chianti? Was he aware that Sirhan Sirhan was in the restroom all along? Is that why he wanted me to keep quiet about his presence in Molly's? Was Nate also part of the conspiracy, or were this photo and letter just his idea of a sick joke? Was it all just a coincidence? *Why had I received this letter?*

Conspiracy or coincidence, I did not care either way. I would never know the answer. I grabbed the envelope, letter, and photograph, and headed for the front door. I took a book of matches from a bowl on the coffee table in the front room. I opened the door, stepped onto the black rubber welcome mat, closed the door, and locked it. I turned around and looked at the neighborhood from the steps of my family's front porch. Two rows of houses with lawns, parked cars, kids on bikes, dogs and cats, a man wearing swimming trunks and combat boots filling a trash can with freshly mowed grass, newspapers on porches. A long way from assassinations or conspiracies.

I ran around the block to St. Andrew's. I went to the church's side door and saw it was open. I went inside and checked to see whether I was alone. I was.

I walked behind the altar and knelt at the foot of the cross where I had seen Karen O'Brien singing a week earlier. I put the letter and photograph back in the envelope and set it on the white marble floor in front of me. I struck a match and set the envelope on fire. I waited until the flames had turned the envelope and its contents to black ashes before leaving God's Chimney.